THE CURSE OF THE MUMMY'S TOMB

Look for more Goosebumps books
by R.L. Stine:

Welcome to Dead House
Stay Out of the Basement
Monster Blood
Say Cheese and Die!

Goosebumps

THE CURSE OF THE MUMMY'S TOMB

R.L. STINE

AN
APPLE
PAPERBACK

SCHOLASTIC INC.
New York Toronto London Auckland Sydney

ISBN 0-590-45369-6

12 11 10 9 8   3 4 5 6 7 8/9

Printed in the U.S.A.   40

First Scholastic printing, January 1993

I saw the Great Pyramid and got thirsty.

Maybe it was all the sand. So dry and yellow, it seemed to stretch on forever. It even made the sky look dry.

I poked my mom in the side. "Mom, I'm really thirsty."

"Not now," she said. She had one hand up on her forehead, shielding her eyes from the bright sun as she stared up at the enormous pyramid.

Not now?

What does "not now" mean? I was thirsty. *Now!*

Someone bumped me from behind and apologized in a foreign language. I never dreamed when I saw the Great Pyramid there'd be so many other tourists. I guess half the people in the world decided to spend their Christmas vacation in Egypt this year.

"But, Mom — " I said. I didn't mean to whine. It was just that my throat was so dry. "I'm really thirsty."

1

"We can't get you a drink now," she answered, staring at the pyramid. "Stop acting like you're four. You're twelve, remember?"

"Twelve-year-olds get thirsty, too," I muttered. "All this sand in the air, it's making me gag."

"Look at the pyramid," she said, sounding a little irritated. "That's why we came here. We didn't come here to get a drink."

"But I'm *choking*!" I cried, gasping and holding my throat.

Okay, so I wasn't choking. I exaggerated a little, just trying to get her attention. But she pulled the brim of her straw hat down and continued to stare up at the pyramid, which shimmered in the heat.

I decided to try my dad. As usual, he was studying the handful of guidebooks he always carried everywhere. I don't think he'd even looked at the pyramid yet. He always misses everything because he always has his nose buried in a guidebook.

"Dad, I'm really thirsty," I said, whispering as if my throat were strained to get my message across.

"Wow. Do you know how wide the pyramid is?" he asked, staring at a picture of the pyramid in his book.

"I'm thirsty, Dad."

"It's thirteen acres wide, Gabe," he said, really

2

excited. "Do you know what it's made of?"

I wanted to say Silly Putty.

He's always testing me. Whenever we go on a trip, he always asks me a million questions like that. I don't think I've ever answered one right.

"Some kind of stone?" I answered.

"That's right." He smiled at me, then turned back to his book. "It's made of limestone. Limestone blocks. It says here that some of the blocks weigh up to a thousand tons."

"Whoa," I said. "That's more than you and Mom put together!"

He turned his eyes from the book and frowned at me. "Not funny, Gabe."

"Just kidding," I said. Dad's a little sensitive about his weight, so I try to tease him about it as often as I can.

"How do you think the ancient Egyptians moved stones that weighed a thousand tons?" he asked.

Quiz time wasn't over.

I took a guess. "In trucks?"

He laughed. "Trucks? They didn't have the *wheel*."

I shielded my eyes and stared up at the pyramid. It was really huge, much bigger than it looks in pictures. And much dryer.

I couldn't imagine how they pulled those big stones across the sand without wheels. "I don't know," I confessed. "I'm really thirsty."

"No one knows how they did it," Dad said.

So it was a trick question.

"Dad, I really need a drink."

"Not now," he said. He squinted at the pyramid. "Gives you a funny feeling, doesn't it?"

"It gives me a thirsty feeling," I said, trying to get my point across.

"No. I mean, it gives me a funny feeling to think that our ancestors — yours and mine, Gabe — may have walked around these pyramids, or even helped to build them. It gives me kind of a chill. How about you?"

"I guess," I told him. He was right. It *was* kind of exciting.

We're Egyptian, you see. I mean, both sets of my grandparents came from Egypt. They moved to the United States around 1930. My mom and dad were both born in Michigan. We were all very excited to see the country our ancestors came from.

"I wonder if your uncle Ben is down inside that pyramid right now," Dad said, shielding his eyes from the sun with one hand.

Uncle Ben Hassad. I had nearly forgotten about my uncle, the famous archaeologist. Uncle Ben was another one of the reasons we had decided to come to Egypt over the holidays. That and the fact that my mom and dad had some business to do in Cairo and Alexandria and some other places.

4

Mom and Dad have their own business. They sell refrigeration equipment. It usually isn't very exciting. But sometimes they travel to neat places, like Egypt, and I get to go with them.

I turned my eyes to the pyramids and thought about my uncle.

Uncle Ben and his workers were digging around in the Great Pyramid, exploring and discovering new mummies, I guess. He had always been fascinated by our ancestors' homeland. He had lived in Egypt for many years. Uncle Ben was an expert on pyramids and mummies. I even saw his picture once in *National Geographic*.

"When are we going to see Uncle Ben?" I asked, tugging Dad's arm. I accidentally tugged too hard, and the guidebooks fell out of his hands.

I helped him pick them up.

"Not today," Dad said, making a face. He didn't like to bend over to pick up things. His stomach got in the way. "Ben's going to meet us in Cairo in a few days."

"Why don't we go up to the pyramid and see if he's there now?" I asked impatiently.

"We're not allowed," Dad replied.

"Look — camels!" Mom poked me on the shoulder and pointed.

Sure enough, some people had arrived on camels. One of the camels seemed to be having a coughing fit. I guess he was thirsty, too. The peo-

5

ple riding the camels were tourists and they looked very uncomfortable. They didn't seem to know what to do next.

"Do you know how to get down from a camel?" I asked my dad.

He was squinting at the pyramid, studying the top of it. "No. How?"

"You don't get down from a camel," I said. "You get down from a duck."

I know. I know. It's a very old joke. But my dad and I never get tired of it.

"Do you see the camels?" Mom asked.

"I'm not blind," I replied. Being thirsty always puts me in a bad mood. Besides, what was so exciting about camels? They were really gross-looking, and they smelled like my gym socks after a basketball game.

"What's your problem?" Mom asked, fiddling with her straw hat.

"I *told* you," I said, not meaning to sound so angry. "I'm thirsty."

"Gabe, really." She glanced at Dad, then went back to staring at the pyramid.

"Dad, do you think Uncle Ben can take us inside the pyramid?" I asked enthusiastically. "That would really be outstanding."

"No, I don't think so," he said. He tucked his guidebooks into his armpit so he could raise his binoculars to his eyes. "I really don't think so, Gabe. I don't think it's allowed."

I couldn't hide my disappointment. I had all these fantasies about going down into the pyramid with my uncle, discovering mummies and ancient treasures. Fighting off ancient Egyptians who had come back to life to defend their sacred tomb, and escaping after a wild chase, just like Indiana Jones.

"I'm afraid you'll just have to appreciate the pyramid from the outside," Dad said, peering over the yellow sand, trying to focus the binoculars.

"I've already appreciated it," I told him glumly. "Can we go get a drink now?"

Little did I know that in a few days, Mom and Dad would be gone, and I would be deep inside the pyramid we were staring at. Not just inside it, but *trapped* inside it, *sealed* inside it — probably forever.

2

We drove from al-Jizah back to Cairo in the funny
little rental car Dad had picked up at the airport.
It wasn't a long drive, but it seemed long to me.
The car was just a little bit bigger than some of
my old remote-control cars, and my head hit the
ceiling with every bump.

I'd brought my Game Boy with me, but Mom
made me put it away so that I could watch the
Nile as the road followed along its bank. It was
very wide and very brown.

"No one else in your class is seeing the Nile this
Christmas," Mom said, the hot wind blowing her
brown hair through the open car window.

"Can I play with my Game Boy now?" I asked.

I mean, when you get right down to it, a river
is a river.

An hour or so later, we were back in Cairo with
its narrow, crowded streets. Dad made a wrong
turn and drove us into some kind of market, and

we were trapped in a little alley behind a herd of goats for nearly half an hour.

I didn't get a drink till we got back to the hotel, and by that time, my tongue was the size of a salami and hanging down to the floor just like Elvis's. He's our cocker spaniel back home.

I'll say one nice thing about Egypt. The Coke tastes just as good as the Coke back home. It's the Classic Coke, too, not the other kind. And they give you plenty of ice, which I like to crunch with my teeth.

We had a suite at the hotel, two bedrooms and a sort of living room. If you looked out the window, you could see a tall, glass skyscraper across the street, just like you'd see in any city.

There was a TV in the living room, but everyone spoke Arabic on it. The shows didn't look too interesting, anyway. Mainly a lot of news. The only channel in English was CNN. But that was news, too.

We had just started to talk about where to go for dinner when the phone rang. Dad went into the bedroom to answer it. A few minutes later he called Mom in, and I could hear the two of them discussing something.

They were talking very quietly, so I figured it had something to do with me and they didn't want me to hear it.

As usual, I was right.

They both came out of the bedroom a few minutes later, looking kind of worried. My first thought was that my grandmother had called to say that something bad had happened to Elvis back home.

"What's wrong?" I asked. "Who called?"

"Your dad and I have to go to Alexandria. Right away," Mom said, sitting down beside me on the couch.

"Huh? Alexandria?" We weren't supposed to go there until the end of the week.

"Business," Dad said. "An important customer wants to meet with us first thing tomorrow morning."

"We have to take a plane that leaves in an hour," Mom said.

"But I don't *want* to," I told them, jumping up from the couch. "I want to stay in Cairo and see Uncle Ben. I want to go to the pyramids with him. You promised!"

We argued about it for a short while. They tried to convince me there were a lot of cool things to see in Alexandria, but I held my ground.

Finally, Mom had an idea. She went into the bedroom, and I heard her making a phone call to someone. A few minutes later, she came back with a smile on her face. "I talked to Uncle Ben," she announced.

"Wow! Do they have phones in the pyramid?" I asked.

"No. I talked to him at the small lodge he's staying at in al-Jizah," she replied. "He said he'd come and take care of you, if you want. While your dad and I are in Alexandria."

"Yeah?" This was starting to sound outstanding. Uncle Ben is one of the coolest guys I've ever known. Sometimes I couldn't believe he was Mom's brother.

"It's your choice, Gabe," she said, glancing at my dad. "You can come with us, or you can stay with Ben till we get back."

Some choice.

I didn't have to think about it for more than one-eighteenth of a second. "I'll stay with Uncle Ben!" I declared.

"One other thing," Mom said, grinning for some reason. "You might want to think about this."

"I don't care *what* it is," I insisted. "I choose Uncle Ben."

"Sari is also on Christmas vacation," Mom said. "And she's staying with him, too."

"Barf!" I cried, and I flung myself down on the couch and began pounding the cushions with both fists.

Sari is Uncle Ben's stuck-up daughter. My only cousin. She's the same age as me — twelve — and she thinks she's so great. She goes to boarding school in the United States while her dad works in Egypt.

She's really pretty, and she knows it. And she's smart. And the last time I saw her, she was an inch taller than me.

That was last Christmas, I guess. She thought she was really hot stuff because she could get to the last level of *Super Mario Land*. But it wasn't fair because I don't have Super Nintendo, only regular Nintendo. So I never get to practice.

I think that's what she liked about me best, that she could beat me at games and things. Sari is the most competitive person I know. She has to be first and best at everything. If everyone around is catching the flu, she has to be the *first* one to catch it!

"Stop pounding the couch like that," Mom said. She grabbed my arm and pulled me to my feet.

"Does that mean you changed your mind? You're coming with us?" Dad asked.

I thought about it. "No. I'll stay here with Uncle Ben," I decided.

"And you won't fight with Sari?" Mom asked.

"She fights with me," I said.

"Your mom and I have got to hurry," Dad said.

They disappeared into the bedroom to pack. I turned on the TV and watched some kind of game show in Arabic. The contestants kept laughing a lot. I couldn't figure out why. I hardly know a word of Arabic.

After a while, Mom and Dad came out again,

dragging suitcases. "We'll never get to the airport in time," Dad said.

"I talked to Ben," Mom told me, brushing her hair with her hand. "He'll be here in an hour, hour and a half. Gabe, you don't mind staying alone here for just an hour, do you?"

"Huh?"

Not much of an answer, I'll admit. But her question caught me by surprise.

I mean, it never occurred to me that my own parents would leave me all alone in a big hotel in a strange city where I didn't even know the language. I mean, how could they do that to me?

"No problem," I said. "I'll be fine. I'll just watch TV till he comes."

"Ben's on his way already," Mom said. "He and Sari will be here in no time. And I phoned down to the hotel manager. He said he'd have someone look in on you from time to time."

"Where's the bellhop?" Dad asked, nervously pacing to the door and back. "I called down there ten minutes ago."

"Just stay here and wait for Ben, okay?" Mom said to me, walking up behind the couch, leaning over, and squeezing my ears. For some reason, she thinks I like that. "Don't go out or anything. Just wait right here for him." She bent down and kissed me on the forehead.

"I won't move," I promised. "I'll stay right here

on the couch. I won't go to the bathroom or anything."

"Can't you ever be serious?" Mom asked, shaking her head.

There was a loud knock on the door. The bellhop, a bent-over old man who didn't look as if he could pick up a feather pillow, had arrived to take the bags.

Mom and Dad, looking very worried, gave me hugs and more final instructions, and told me once again to stay in the room. The door closed behind them, and it was suddenly very quiet.

Very quiet.

I turned up the TV just to make it a little noisier. The game show had gone off, and now a man in a white suit was reading the news in Arabic.

"I'm not scared," I said aloud. But I had kind of a tight feeling in my throat.

I walked to the window and looked out. The sun was nearly down. The shadow of the skyscraper slanted over the street and onto the hotel.

I picked up my Coke glass and took a sip. It was watery and flat. My stomach growled. I suddenly realized that I was hungry.

Room service, I thought.

Then I decided I'd better not. What if I called and they only spoke Arabic?

I glanced at the clock. Seven-twenty. I wished Uncle Ben would arrive.

14

I wasn't scared. I just wished he'd arrive.

Okay. Maybe I was a little nervous.

I paced back and forth for a bit. I tried playing *Tetris* on the Game Boy, but I couldn't concentrate, and the light wasn't very good.

Sari is probably a champ at *Tetris*, I thought bitterly. Where *were* they? What was taking so long?

I began to have horrible, frightening thoughts: What if they can't find the hotel? What if they get mixed up and go to the wrong hotel?

What if they're in a terrible car crash and die? And I'm all by myself in Cairo for days and days?

I know. They were dumb thoughts. But they're the kind of thoughts you have when you're alone in a strange place, waiting for someone to come.

I glanced down and realized I had taken the mummy hand out of my jeans pocket.

It was small, the size of a child's hand. A little hand wrapped in papery brown gauze. I had bought it at a garage sale a few years ago, and I always carried it around as a good luck charm.

The kid who sold it to me called it a "Summoner." He said it was used to summon evil spirits, or something. I didn't care about that. I just thought it was an outstanding bargain for two dollars. I mean, what a great thing to find at a garage sale! And maybe it was even real.

I tossed it from hand to hand as I paced the length of the living room. The TV was starting to make me nervous, so I clicked it off.

But now the quiet was making me nervous.

I slapped the mummy hand against my palm and kept pacing.

Where were they? They should've been here by now.

I was beginning to think that I'd made the wrong choice. Maybe I should've gone to Alexandria with Mom and Dad.

Then I heard a noise at the door. Footsteps.

Was it them?

I stopped in the middle of the living room and listened, staring past the narrow front hallway to the door.

The light was dim in the hallway, but I saw the doorknob turn.

That's strange, I thought. Uncle Ben would knock first — wouldn't he?

The doorknob turned. The door started to creak open.

"Hey — " I called out, but the word choked in my throat.

Uncle Ben would knock. He wouldn't just barge in.

Slowly, slowly, the door squeaked open as I stared, frozen in the middle of the room, unable to call out.

Standing in the doorway was a tall, shadowy figure.

I gasped as the figure lurched into the room,

and I saw it clearly. Even in the dim light, I could see what it was.

A mummy.

Glaring at me with round, dark eyes through holes in its ancient, thick bandages.

A mummy.

Pushing itself off the wall and staggering stiffly toward me into the living room, its arms outstretched as if to grab me.

I opened my mouth to scream, but no sound came out.

3

I took a step back, and then another. Without realizing it, I'd raised my little mummy hand in the air, as if trying to fend off the intruder with it.

As the mummy staggered into the light, I stared into its deep, dark eyes.

And recognized them.

"Uncle Ben!" I screamed.

Angrily, I heaved the mummy hand at him. It hit his bandaged chest and bounced off.

He collapsed backwards against the wall, laughing that booming laugh of his.

And then I saw Sari poking her head in the doorway. She was laughing, too.

They both thought it was hilarious. But my heart was pounding so hard, I thought it was going to pop out of my chest.

"That wasn't funny!" I shouted angrily, balling my hands into fists at my sides. I took a deep breath, then another, trying to get my breathing to return to normal.

"I told you he'd be scared," Sari said, walking into the room, a big, superior grin on her face.

Uncle Ben was laughing so hard, he had tears running down his bandaged face. He was a big man, tall and broad, and his laughter shook the room. "You weren't that scared — were you, Gabe?"

"I knew it was you," I said, my heart still pounding as if it were a windup toy someone had wound up too tight. "I recognized you right away."

"You sure *looked* scared," Sari insisted.

"I didn't want to spoil the joke," I replied, wondering if they could see how terrified I really was.

"You should've seen the look on your face!" Uncle Ben cried, and started laughing all over again.

"I told Daddy he shouldn't do it," Sari said, dropping down onto the couch. "I'm amazed the hotel people let him come up dressed like that."

Uncle Ben bent down and picked up the mummy hand I had tossed at him. "You're used to me and my practical jokes, right, Gabe?"

"Yeah," I said, avoiding his eyes.

Secretly, I scolded myself for falling for his stupid costume. I was always falling for his dumb jokes. Always. And, now, there was Sari grinning at me from the couch, knowing I was so scared that I'd practically had a cow.

Uncle Ben pulled some of the bandages away from his face. He stepped over and handed the little mummy hand back to me. "Where'd you get that?" he asked.

"Garage sale," I told him.

I started to ask him if it was real, but he surrounded me in a big bear hug. The gauze felt rough against my cheek. "Good to see you, Gabe," he said softly. "You've grown taller."

"Almost as tall as me," Sari chimed in.

Uncle Ben motioned to her. "Get up and help me pull this stuff off."

"I kind of like the way you look in it," Sari said.

"Get over here," Uncle Ben insisted.

Sari got up with a sigh, tossing her straight black hair behind her shoulders. She walked over to her dad and started unraveling the bandages.

"I got a little carried away with this mummy thing, Gabe," Uncle Ben admitted, resting his arm on my shoulder as Sari continued working. "But it's just because I'm so excited about what's going on at the pyramid."

"What's going on?" I asked eagerly.

"Daddy's discovered a whole new burial chamber," Sari broke in before her dad had a chance to tell me himself. "He's exploring parts of the pyramid that have been undiscovered for thousands of years."

"Really?" I cried. "That's outstanding!"

Uncle Ben chuckled. "Wait till you see it."

"See it?" I wasn't sure what he meant. "You mean you're going to take me into the pyramid?"

My voice was so high that only dogs could hear it. But I didn't care. I couldn't believe my good luck. I was actually going inside the Great Pyramid, into a section that hadn't been discovered until now.

"I have no choice," Uncle Ben said dryly. "What else am I going to do with you two?"

"Are there mummies in there?" I asked. "Will we see actual mummies?"

"Do you miss your mummy?" Sari said, her lame idea of a joke.

I ignored her. "Is there treasure down there, Uncle Ben? Egyptian relics? Are there wall paintings?"

"Let's talk about it at dinner," he said, tugging off the last of the bandages. He was wearing a plaid sportshirt and baggy chinos under all the gauze. "Come on. I'm starving."

"Race you downstairs," Sari said, and shoved me out of the way to give herself a good head start out of the room.

We ate downstairs in the hotel restaurant. There were palm trees painted on the walls, and miniature palm trees planted in big pots all around the restaurant. Large wooden ceiling fans whirled slowly overhead.

The three of us sat in a large booth, Sari and I

21

across from Uncle Ben. We studied the long menus. They were printed in Arabic and English.

"Listen to this, Gabe," Sari said, a smug smile on her face. She began to read the Arabic words aloud.

What a show-off.

The white-suited waiter brought a basket of flat pita bread and a bowl of green stuff to dip the bread in. I ordered a club sandwich and French fries. Sari ordered a hamburger.

Later, as we ate our dinner, Uncle Ben explained a little more about what he had discovered at the pyramid. "As you probably know," he started, tearing off a chunk of the flat bread, "the pyramid was built some time around 2500 B.C., during the reign of the Pharaoh Khufu."

"*Gesundheit,*" Sari said. Another lame joke.

Her father chuckled. I made a face at her.

"It was the biggest structure of its time," Uncle Ben said. "Do you know how wide the base of the pyramid is?"

Sari shook her head. "No. How wide?" she asked with a mouthful of hamburger.

"I know," I said, grinning. "It's thirteen acres wide."

"Hey — that's right!" Uncle Ben exclaimed, obviously impressed.

Sari flashed me a surprised look.

That's one for me! I thought happily, sticking my tongue out at her.

And one for my dad's guidebooks.

"The pyramid was built as a royal burial place," Uncle Ben continued, his expression turning serious. "The Pharaoh made it really enormous so that the burial chamber could be hidden. The Egyptians worried about tomb robbers. They knew that people would try to break in and take all of the valuable jewels and treasures that were buried alongside their owners. So they built dozens of tunnels and chambers inside, a confusing maze to keep robbers from finding the real burial room."

"Pass the ketchup, please," Sari interrupted. I passed her the ketchup.

"Sari's heard all this before," Uncle Ben said, dipping the pita bread into the dark gravy on his plate. "Anyway, we archaeologists thought we'd uncovered all of the tunnels and rooms inside this pyramid. But a few days ago, my workers and I discovered a tunnel that isn't on any of the charts. An unexplored, undiscovered tunnel. And we think this tunnel may lead us to the actual burial chamber of Khufu himself!"

"Outstanding!" I exclaimed. "And Sari and I will be there when you discover it?"

Uncle Ben chuckled. "I don't know about that, Gabe. It may take us years of careful exploration. But I'll take you down into the tunnel tomorrow. Then you can tell your friends you were actually inside the ancient pyramid of Khufu."

"I've already been in it," Sari bragged. She

turned her eyes to me. "It's very dark. You might get scared."

"No, I won't," I insisted. "No way."

The three of us spent the night in my parents' hotel room. It took me hours to get to sleep. I guess I was excited about going into the pyramid. I kept imagining that we found mummies and big chests of ancient jewels and treasure.

Uncle Ben woke us up early the next morning, and we drove out to the pyramid outside al-Jizah. The air was already hot and sticky. The sun seemed to hang low over the desert like an orange balloon.

"There it is!" Sari declared, pointing out the window. And I saw the Great Pyramid rising up from the yellow sand like some kind of mirage.

Uncle Ben showed a special permit to the blue-uniformed guard, and we followed a narrow, private road that curved through the sand behind the pyramid. We parked beside several other cars and vans in the blue-gray shadow of the pyramid.

As I stepped out of the car, my chest was thudding with excitement. I stared up at the enormous, worn stones of the Great Pyramid.

It's over four thousand years old, I thought. I'm about to go inside something that was built four thousand years ago!

"Your sneaker's untied," Sari said, pointing.

She sure knew how to bring a guy back down to earth.

I bent in the sand to tie my sneaker. For some reason, the left one was always coming untied, even when I double-knotted it.

"My workers are already inside," Uncle Ben told us. "Now, stick close together, okay? Don't wander off. The tunnels really are like a maze. It's very easy to get lost."

"No problem," I said, my trembling voice revealing how nervous and excited I was.

"Don't worry. I'll keep an eye on Gabe, Dad," Sari said.

She was only two months older than me. Why did she have to act like she was my baby-sitter or something?

Uncle Ben handed us both flashlights. "Clip them onto your jeans as we go in," he instructed. He gazed at me. "You don't believe in curses, do you? You know — the ancient Egyptian kind."

I didn't know how to reply, so I shook my head.

"Good," Uncle Ben replied, grinning. "Because one of my workers claims we've violated an ancient decree by entering this new tunnel, and that we've activated some curse."

"We're not scared," Sari said, giving him a playful shove toward the entrance. "Get going, Dad."

And seconds later, we were stepping into the small, square opening cut into the stone. Stooping

25

low, I followed them through a narrow tunnel that seemed to slope gradually down.

Uncle Ben led the way, lighting the ground with a bright halogen flashlight. The pyramid floor was soft and sandy. The air was cool and damp.

"The walls are granite," Uncle Ben said, stopping to rub a hand along the low ceiling. "All of the tunnels were made of limestone."

The temperature dropped suddenly. The air felt even wetter. I suddenly realized why Uncle Ben had made us wear our sweatshirts.

"If you're scared, we can go back," Sari said.

"I'm fine," I replied quickly.

The tunnel ended abruptly. A pale yellow wall rose up in front of us. Ben's flashlight darted over a small, dark hole in the floor.

"Down we go," Ben said, groaning as he dropped to his knees. He turned back to me. "Afraid there are no stairs down to the new tunnel. My workers installed a rope ladder. Just take your time on it, take it slowly, one rung at a time, and you'll be fine."

"No problem," I said. But my voice cracked.

"Don't look down," Sari advised. "It might make you dizzy, and you'll fall."

"Thanks for the encouragement," I told her. I pushed my way past her. "I'll go down first," I said. I was already tired of her acting so superior. I decided to show her who was brave and who wasn't.

"No. Let me go first," Uncle Ben said, raising a hand to stop me. "Then I'll shine the light up at the ladder and help you down."

With another groan, he maneuvered himself into the hole. He was so big, he nearly didn't fit.

Slowly, he began to lower himself down the rope ladder.

Sari and I leaned over the hole and peered down, watching him descend. The rope ladder wasn't very steady. It swung back and forth under his weight as he slowly, carefully, made his way down.

"It's a long way down," I said softly.

Sari didn't reply. In the shadowy light, I could see her worried expression. She was chewing on her lower lip as her dad reached the tunnel floor.

She was nervous, too.

That cheered me up a lot.

"Okay, I'm down. You're next, Gabe," Uncle Ben called up to me.

I turned and swung my feet onto the rope ladder. I grinned at Sari. "See ya."

I lowered my hands to the sides of the rope ladder — and as I slid them down, I cried out.

"Ow!"

The rope wasn't smooth. It was coarse. It cut my hands.

The sharp stab of pain made me lift my hands.

And before I even realized what was happening, I started to fall.

4

Two hands reached down for mine. They shot through the air and grabbed my wrists.

"Hold on!" Sari cried.

She had slowed my fall just enough to allow me to grab back onto the sides of the rope ladder.

"Oh, wow!" I managed to utter. That was the best I could do. I gripped the rope for dear life, waiting for my heart to stop pounding. I closed my eyes and didn't move. I squeezed the ropes so hard, my hands ached.

"Saved your life," Sari called down to me, leaning into the opening, her face inches from mine.

I opened my eyes and stared up at her. "Thanks," I said gratefully.

"No problem," she replied and burst out laughing, laughing from relief, I guess.

Why couldn't I save *her* life? I asked myself angrily. Why can't *I* ever be the big hero?

"What happened, Gabe?" Uncle Ben called from the tunnel floor below. His booming voice echoed loudly through the chamber. The wide circle of light from his flashlight danced across the granite wall.

"The rope cut my hands," I explained. "I wasn't expecting — "

"Just take your time," he said patiently. "One rung at a time, remember?"

"Lower your hands. Don't slide them," Sari advised, her face poking through the hole above me.

"Okay, okay," I said, starting to breathe normally.

I took a deep breath and held it. Then, slowly, carefully, I made my way down the long rope ladder.

A short while later, all three of us were standing on the tunnel floor, holding our lighted flashlights, our eyes following the circles of light. "This way," Uncle Ben said quietly, and he headed off to the right, walking slowly, stooping because of the low ceiling.

Our sneakers crunched on the sandy floor. I saw another tunnel leading off to the right, then another tunnel on the left.

"We're breathing air that is four thousand years old," Ben said, keeping his light aimed on the floor ahead of him.

"Smells like it," I whispered to Sari. She laughed.

The air really did smell old. Kind of heavy and musty. Like someone's attic.

The tunnel widened a little as it curved to the right.

"We're going deeper into the earth," Ben said. "Does it feel like you're going downhill?"

Sari and I both muttered that it did.

"Dad and I explored one of the side tunnels yesterday," Sari told me. "We found a mummy case inside a tiny room. A beautiful one in perfect condition."

"Was there a mummy inside it?" I asked eagerly. I was dying to see a mummy. The museum back home had only one. I'd stared at it and studied it all my life.

"No. It was empty," Sari replied.

"Why didn't the mummy have any hobbies?" Uncle Ben asked, stopping suddenly.

"I don't know," I answered.

"He was too wrapped up in his work!" Uncle Ben exclaimed. He laughed at his own joke. Sari and I could only muster weak smiles.

"Don't encourage him," Sari told me, loud enough for her dad to hear. "He knows a million mummy jokes, and they're all just as bad."

"Wait up. Just a sec," I said. I bent down to tie my sneaker, which had come undone again.

The tunnel curved, then divided into two tunnels. Uncle Ben led us through the one on the left, which was so narrow we had to squeeze through it, making our way sideways, heads bent, until it widened into a large, high-ceilinged chamber.

I stood up straight and stretched. It felt so good not to be scrunched down. I stared around the large room.

Several people came into view at the far wall, working with digging tools. Bright spotlights had been hung above them on the wall, attached to a portable generator.

Uncle Ben brought us over to them and introduced us. There were four workers, two men and two women.

Another man stood off to the side, a clipboard in his hand. He was an Egyptian, dressed all in white except for a red bandanna around his neck. He had straight black hair, slicked down and tied in a ponytail behind his head. He stared at Sari and me, but didn't come over. He seemed to be studying us.

"Ahmed, you met my daughter yesterday. This is Gabe, my nephew," Uncle Ben called to him.

Ahmed nodded, but didn't smile or say anything.

"Ahmed is from the university," Uncle Ben explained to me in a low voice. "He requested permission to observe us, and I said okay. He's very quiet. But don't get him started on ancient curses. He's the one who keeps warning me that I'm in deadly danger."

Ahmed nodded, but didn't reply. He stared at me for a long while.

Weird guy, I thought.

I wondered if he'd tell me about the ancient curses. I loved stories about ancient curses.

Uncle Ben turned to his workers. "So? Any progress today?" he asked.

"We think we're getting real close," a young, red-haired man wearing faded jeans and a blue denim work shirt replied. And then he added, "Just a hunch."

Ben frowned. "Thanks, Quasimodo," he said.

The workers all laughed. I guess they liked Uncle Ben's jokes.

"Quasimodo was the Hunchback of Notre Dame," Sari explained to me in her superior tone.

"I know, I know," I replied irritably. "I get it."

"We could be heading in the wrong direction altogether," Uncle Ben told the workers, scratching the bald spot on the back of his head. "The tunnel might be over there." He pointed to the wall on the right.

"No, I think we're getting warm, Ben," a young woman, her face smudged with dust, said. "Come over here. I want to show you something."

She led him over to a large pile of stones and debris. He shined his light where she was pointing. Then he leaned closer to examine what she was showing him.

"That's very interesting, Christy," Uncle Ben said, rubbing his chin. They fell into a long discussion.

After a while, three other workers entered the

chamber, carrying shovels and picks. One of them was carrying some kind of electronic equipment in a flat metal case. It looked a little like a laptop computer.

I wanted to ask Uncle Ben what it was, but he was still in the corner, involved in his discussion with the worker named Christy.

Sari and I wandered back toward the tunnel entrance. "I think he's forgotten about us," Sari said sullenly.

I agreed, shining my flashlight up at the high, cracked ceiling.

"Once he gets down here with the workers, he forgets everything but his work," she said, sighing.

"I can't believe we're actually inside a pyramid!" I exclaimed.

Sari laughed. She kicked at the floor with one sneaker. "Look — ancient dirt," she said.

"Yeah." I kicked up some of the sandy dirt, too. "I wonder who walked here last. Maybe an Egyptian priestess. Maybe a pharaoh. They might have stood right here on this spot."

"Let's go exploring," Sari said suddenly.

"Huh?"

Her dark eyes gleamed, and she had a really devilish look on her face. "Let's go, Gabey — let's check out some tunnels or something."

"Don't call me Gabey," I said. "Come on, Sari, you know I hate that."

"Sorry," she apologized, giggling. "You coming?"

"We can't," I insisted, watching Uncle Ben. He was having some kind of argument with the worker carrying the thing that looked like a laptop. "Your dad said we had to stick together. He said — "

"He'll be busy here for hours," she interrupted, glancing back at him. "He won't even notice we're gone. Really."

"But, Sari — " I started.

"Besides," she continued, putting her hands on my shoulders and pushing me backwards toward the chamber door, "he doesn't want us hanging around. We'll only get in the way."

"Sari — "

"I went exploring yesterday," she said, pushing me with both hands. "We won't go far. You can't get lost. All the tunnels lead back to this big room. Really."

"I just don't think we should," I said, my eyes on Uncle Ben. He was down on his hands and knees now, digging against the wall with some kind of a pick.

"Let go of me," I told her. "Really. I — "

And then she said what I knew she'd say. What she *always* says when she wants to get her way.

"Are you chicken?"

"No," I insisted. "You know your dad said — "

"Chicken? Chicken? Chicken?" She began clucking like a chicken. Really obnoxious.

"Stop it, Sari." I tried to sound tough and menacing.

"Are you chicken, *Gabey*?" she repeated, grinning at me as if she'd just won some big victory. "Huh, *Gabey*?"

"Stop calling me that!" I insisted.

She just stared at me.

I made a disgusted face. "Okay, okay. Let's go exploring," I told her.

I mean, what else could I say?

"But not far," I added.

"Don't worry," she said, grinning. "We won't get lost. I'll just show you some of the tunnels I looked at yesterday. One of them has a strange animal picture carved on the wall. I think it's some kind of a cat. I'm not sure."

"Really?" I cried, instantly excited. "I've seen pictures of relief carvings, but I've never — "

"It may be a cat," Sari said. "Or maybe a person with an animal head. It's really weird."

"Where is it?" I asked.

"Follow me."

We both gave one last glance back to Uncle Ben, who was down on his hands and knees, picking away at the stone wall.

Then I followed Sari out of the chamber.

We squeezed through the narrow tunnel, then turned and followed a slightly wider tunnel to the right. I hesitated, a few steps behind her. "Are

35

you sure we'll be able to get back?" I asked, keeping my voice low so she couldn't accuse me of sounding frightened.

"No problem," she replied. "Keep your light on the floor. There's a small chamber on the other end of this tunnel that's kind of neat."

We followed the tunnel as it curved to the right. It branched into two low openings, and Sari took the one to the left.

The air grew a little warmer. It smelled stale, as if people had been smoking cigarettes there.

This tunnel was wider than the others. Sari was walking faster now, getting farther ahead of me. "Hey — wait up!" I cried.

I looked down to see that my sneaker had come untied again. Uttering a loud, annoyed groan, I bent to retie it.

"Hey, Sari, wait up!"

She didn't seem to hear me.

I could see her light in the distance, growing fainter in the tunnel.

Then it suddenly disappeared.

Had her flashlight burned out?

No. The tunnel probably curved, I decided. She's just out of my view.

"Hey, Sari!" I called. "Wait up! Wait *up*!"

I stared ahead into the dark tunnel.

"Sari?"

Why didn't she answer me?

5

"Sari!"

My voice echoed through the long, curving tunnel.

No reply.

I called again, and listened to my voice fading as the echo repeated her name again and again.

At first I was angry.

I knew what Sari was doing.

She was deliberately not answering, deliberately trying to frighten me.

She had to prove that she was the brave one, and I was the 'fraidy cat.

I suddenly remembered another time, a few years before. Sari and Uncle Ben had come to my house for a visit. I think Sari and I were seven or eight.

We went outside to play. It was a gray day, threatening rain. Sari had a jump rope and was showing off, as usual, showing me how good she was at it. Then, of course, when she let me try it, I tripped and fell, and she laughed like crazy.

I'd decided to get back at her by taking her to this deserted old house a couple blocks up the street. The kids in the neighborhood all believed the house was haunted. It was a neat place to sneak in and explore, although our parents were always warning us to stay away from it because it was falling apart and dangerous.

So I led Sari to this house and told her it was haunted. And we sneaked in through the broken basement window.

It got even darker out, and started to rain. It was perfect. I could tell Sari was really scared to be alone in the creepy old house. I, of course, wasn't scared at all because I'd been there before.

Well, we started exploring, with me leading the way. And somehow we got separated. And it started thundering and lightning outside. There was rain pouring in through the broken windows.

I decided maybe we should get home. So I called to Sari. No answer.

I called again. Still no answer.

Then I heard a loud crash.

Calling her name, I started running from room to room. I was scared to death. I was sure something terrible had happened.

I ran through every room in the house, getting more and more scared. I couldn't find her. I shouted and shouted, but she didn't answer me.

I was so scared, I started to cry. Then I totally

panicked, and I ran out of the house and into the pouring rain.

I ran through the thunder and lightning, crying all the way home. By the time I got home, I was soaked through and through.

I ran into the kitchen, sobbing and crying that I'd lost Sari in the haunted house.

And there she was. Sitting at the kitchen table. Comfortable and dry. Eating a big slice of chocolate cake. A smug smile on her face.

And now, peering into the darkness of the pyramid, I knew Sari was doing the same thing to me.

Trying to scare me.

Trying to make me look bad.

Or *was* she?

As I made my way through the low, narrow tunnel, keeping the light aimed straight ahead, I couldn't help it. My anger quickly turned to worry, and troubling questions whirred through my mind.

What if she *wasn't* playing a mean trick on me?

What if something bad *had* happened to her?

What if she had missed a step and fallen into a hole?

Or had gotten herself trapped in a hidden tunnel? Or . . . I didn't know what.

I wasn't thinking clearly.

My sneakers thudded loudly over the sandy floor as I started to half-walk, half-jog through the winding tunnel. "Sari?" I called, frantically now, not caring whether I sounded frightened or not.

Where was she?

She wasn't that far ahead of me. I should at least be able to see the light from her flashlight, I thought.

"Sari?"

There was no place for her to hide in this narrow space. Was I following the wrong tunnel?

No.

I had been in the same tunnel all along. The same tunnel I had watched her disappear in.

Don't say *disappear*, I scolded myself. Don't even *think* the word.

Suddenly the narrow tunnel ended. A small opening led into a small, square room. I flashed the light quickly from side to side.

"Sari?"

No sign of her.

The walls were bare. The air was warm and stale. I moved the flashlight rapidly across the floor, looking for Sari's footprints. The floor was harder, less sandy here. There were no footprints.

"Oh!"

I uttered a low cry when my light came to rest on the object against the far wall. My heart pounding, I eagerly took a few steps closer until I was just a few feet from it.

It was a mummy case.

A large, stone mummy case, at least eight feet long.

It was rectangular, with curved corners. The lid was carved. I stepped closer and aimed the light.

Yes.

A human face was carved on the lid. The face of a woman. It looked like a death mask, the kind we'd studied in school. It stared wide-eyed up at the ceiling.

"Wow!" I cried aloud. A real mummy case.

The carved face on the lid must have been brightly painted at one time. But the color had faded over the centuries. Now the face was gray, as pale as death.

Staring at the top of the case, smooth and perfect, I wondered if Uncle Ben had seen it. Or if I had made a discovery of my own.

Why is it all by itself in this small room? I wondered.

And what does it hold inside?

I was working up my courage to run my hand over the smooth stone of the lid when I heard the creaking sound.

And saw the lid start to raise up.

"Oh!" a hushed cry escaped my lips.

At first I thought I had imagined it. I didn't move a muscle. I kept the light trained on the lid.

The lid lifted a tiny bit more.

And I heard a hissing sound come from inside

the big coffin, like air escaping a new coffee can when you first open it.

Uttering another low cry, I took a step back.

The lid raised up another inch.

I took another step back.

And dropped the flashlight.

I picked it up with a trembling hand and shined it back onto the mummy case.

The lid was now open nearly a foot.

I sucked in a deep breath of air and held it.

I wanted to run, but my fear was freezing me in place.

I wanted to scream, but I knew I wouldn't be able to make a sound.

The lid creaked and opened another inch.

Another inch.

I lowered the flashlight to the opening, the light quivering with my hand.

From the dark depths of the ancient coffin, I saw two eyes staring out at me.

6

I uttered a silent gasp.

I froze.

I felt a cold chill zigzag down my back.

The lid slowly pushed open another inch.

The eyes stared out at me. Cold eyes. Evil eyes. Ancient eyes.

My mouth dropped open. And before I even realized it, I started to scream.

Scream at the top of my lungs.

As I screamed, unable to turn away, unable to run, unable to move, the lid slid open all the way.

Slowly, as if in a dream, a dark figure raised itself from the depths of the mummy case and climbed out.

"*Sari!*"

A broad smile widened across her face. Her eyes glowed gleefully.

"Sari — that wasn't funny!" I managed to shout in a high-pitched voice that bounced off the stone walls.

But now she was laughing too hard to hear me. Loud, scornful laughter.

I was so furious, I searched frantically for something to throw at her. But there wasn't anything, not even a pebble on the floor.

Staring at her, my chest still heaving from my fright, I really hated her then. She had made a total fool of me. There I had been, screaming like a baby.

I knew she'd never let me live it down.

Never.

"The look on your face!" she exclaimed when she finally stopped laughing. "I wish I had a camera."

I was too angry to reply. I just growled at her.

I pulled the little mummy hand from my back pocket and began rolling it around in my hand. I always fiddled with that hand when I was upset. It usually helped to calm me.

But now I felt as if I'd *never* calm down.

"I *told* you I'd found an empty mummy case yesterday," she said, brushing the hair back off her face. "Didn't you remember?"

I growled again.

I felt like a total dork.

First I'd fallen for her dad's stupid mummy costume. And now this.

Silently to myself I vowed to pay her back. If it was the last thing I ever did.

She was still chuckling about her big-deal joke.

"The look on your face," she said again, shaking her head. Rubbing it in.

"You wouldn't like it if I scared you," I muttered angrily.

"You *couldn't* scare me," she replied. "I don't scare so easy."

"Hah!"

That was the best comeback I could think of. Not very clever, I know. But I was too angry to be clever.

I was imagining myself picking Sari up and tossing her back into the mummy case, pulling down the lid, and locking it — when I heard footsteps approaching in the tunnel.

Glancing over at Sari, I saw her expression change. She heard them, too.

A few seconds later, Uncle Ben burst into the small room. I could see immediately, even in the dim light, that he was really angry.

"I thought I could trust you two," he said, talking through gritted teeth.

"Dad — " Sari started.

But he cut her off sharply. "I trusted you not to wander off without telling me. Do you know how easy it is to get lost in this place? Lost forever?"

"Dad," Sari started again. "I was just showing Gabe this room I discovered yesterday. We were going to come right back. Really."

"There are *hundreds* of tunnels," Uncle Ben

said heatedly, ignoring Sari's explanation. "Maybe thousands. Many of them have never been explored. No one has ever been in this section of the pyramid before. We have no idea what dangers there are. You two can't just wander off by yourselves. Do you know how frantic I was when I turned around and you were gone?"

"Sorry," Sari and I both said in unison.

"Let's go," Uncle Ben said, gesturing to the door with his flashlight. "Your pyramid visit is over for today."

We followed him into the tunnel. I felt really bad. Not only had I fallen for Sari's stupid joke, but I'd made my favorite uncle really angry.

Sari always gets me into trouble, I thought bitterly. Since we were little kids.

Now she was walking ahead of me, arm in arm with her dad, telling him something, her face close to his ear. Suddenly they both burst out laughing and turned back to look at me.

I could feel my face getting hot.

I knew what she'd told him.

She'd told him about hiding in the mummy case and making me scream like a scared baby. And now they were both chuckling about what a jerk I was.

"Merry Christmas to you, too!" I called bitterly.

And that made them laugh even harder.

* * *

We spent the night back in the hotel in Cairo. I beat Sari in two straight games of Scrabble, but it didn't make me feel any better.

She kept complaining that she had only vowels, and so the games weren't fair. Finally, I put my Scrabble set back in my room, and we sat and stared at the TV.

The next morning, we had breakfast in the room. I ordered pancakes, but they didn't taste like any pancakes I'd ever eaten. They were tough and grainy, as if they were made of cowhide or something.

"What are we doing today?" Sari asked Uncle Ben, who was still yawning and stretching after two cups of black coffee.

"I have an appointment at the Cairo Museum," he told us, glancing at his wristwatch. "It's just a couple of blocks away. I thought you two might like to wander around the museum while I have my meeting."

"Ooh, thrills and chills," Sari said sarcastically. She slurped up another spoonful of Frosted Flakes.

The little Frosted Flakes box had Arabic writing all over it, and Tony the Tiger was saying something in Arabic. I wanted to save it and take it home to show my friends. But I knew Sari would make fun of me if I asked her for it, so I didn't.

"The museum has an interesting mummy collection, Gabe," Uncle Ben said to me. He tried to pour himself a third cup of coffee, but the pot was empty. "You'll like it."

"Unless they climb out of their cases," Sari said. Lame. Really lame.

I stuck my tongue out at her. She tossed a wet Frosted Flake across the table at me.

"When are my mom and dad getting back?" I asked Uncle Ben. I suddenly realized I missed them.

He started to answer, but the phone rang. He walked into the bedroom and picked it up. It was an old-fashioned black telephone with a dial instead of buttons. As he talked, his face filled with concern.

"Change of plans," he said a few seconds later, hanging up the receiver and coming back into the living room.

"What's the matter, Daddy?" Sari asked, shoving her cereal bowl away.

"It's very strange," he replied, scratching the back of his head. "Two of my workers came down sick last night. Some kind of mysterious illness." His expression became thoughtful, worried. "They took them to a hospital here in Cairo."

He started to gather up his wallet and some other belongings. "I think I'd better get over there right away," he said.

"But what about Gabe and me?" Sari asked, glancing at me.

"I'll only be gone an hour or so," her dad replied. "Stay here in the room, okay?"

"In the *room*?" Sari cried, making it sound like a punishment.

"Well, okay. You can go down to the lobby, if you want. But don't leave the hotel."

A few minutes later, he pulled on his tan safari jacket, checked one last time to make sure he had his wallet and keys, and hurried out the door.

Sari and I stared at each other glumly. "What do you want to do?" I asked, poking the cold, uneaten pancakes on my plate with a fork.

Sari shrugged. "Is it hot in here?"

I nodded. "Yeah. It's about a hundred and twenty."

"We have to get out of here," she said, standing up and stretching.

"You mean go down to the lobby?" I asked, still poking the pancakes, pulling them into pieces with the fork.

"No. I mean get *out* of here," she replied. She walked over to the mirror in the entranceway and began brushing her straight, black hair.

"But Uncle Ben said — " I started.

"We won't go far," she said, and then quickly added, "if you're afraid."

I made a face at her. I don't think she saw me. She was busy admiring herself in the mirror.

"Okay," I told her. "We could go to the museum. Your dad said it was just a block away."

I was determined not to be the wimp anymore. If she wanted to disobey her dad and go out, fine with me. From now on, I decided, *I'll* be the macho guy. No repeats of yesterday — ever again.

"The museum?" She made a face. "Well . . . okay," she said, turning to look at me. "We're twelve, after all. It's not like we're babies. We can go out if we want."

"Yes, we can," I said. "I'll write Uncle Ben a note and tell him where we're going, in case he gets back before we do." I went over to the desk and picked up a pen and a small pad of paper.

"If you're afraid, *Gabey*, we can just walk around the block," she said in a teasing voice, staring at me, waiting to see how I'd react.

"No way," I said. "We're going to the museum. Unless *you're* afraid."

"No way," she said, imitating me.

"And don't call me Gabey," I added.

"Gabey, Gabey, Gabey," she muttered, just to be annoying.

I wrote the note to Uncle Ben. Then we took the elevator down to the lobby. We asked a young woman behind the desk where the Cairo Museum was. She said to turn right outside the hotel and walk two blocks.

Sari hesitated as we stepped out into the bright sunshine. "You sure you're up for this?"

"What could go wrong?" I replied.

7

"Let's go. This way," I said, shielding my eyes from the bright sunlight with my hand.

"It's so hot," Sari complained.

The street was crowded and noisy. I couldn't hear anything over the honking of car horns.

Drivers here lean on their horns the minute they start up their cars, and they don't stop honking till they arrive at their destinations.

Sari and I stayed close together, making our way through the crush of people on the sidewalk. All kinds of people passed by.

There were men in American-style business suits walking alongside men who appeared to be wearing loose-fitting white pajamas.

We saw women who would look right at home on any street in America, wearing colorful leggings and stylish skirts and slacks. Women in jeans. Followed by women dressed in long, flowing black dresses, their faces covered by heavy, black veils.

"This sure doesn't look like back home!" I exclaimed, shouting over the blare of car horns.

I was so fascinated by all the interesting-looking people crowding the narrow sidewalk that I forgot to look at the buildings. Before I knew it, we were standing in front of the museum, a tall, stone structure looming above the street behind steeply sloping steps.

We climbed the steps and entered the revolving door of the museum.

"Wow, it's so quiet in here!" I exclaimed, whispering. It was nice to get away from the honking horns, the crowded sidewalks, and shouting people.

"Why do you think they honk their horns so much?" Sari asked, holding her ears.

"Just a custom, I guess," I replied.

We stopped and looked around.

We were standing in the center of an enormous open lobby. Tall marble stairways rose up on the far left and far right. Twin white columns framed a wide doorway that led straight back. An enormous mural across the wall to the right showed an aerial view of the pyramids and the Nile.

We stood in the middle of the floor, admiring the mural for a while. Then we made our way to the back wall and asked a woman at the information desk for the mummy room. She flashed us a nice smile and told us in perfect English to take the stairs to the right.

Our sneakers thudded loudly over the shiny

marble floor. The stairway seemed to go up forever. "This is like mountain climbing," I complained, halfway up.

"Race you to the top," Sari said, grinning, and took off before I had a chance to reply.

Of course she beat me by about ten steps.

I waited for her to call me "slowpoke" or "snail face" or something. But she had already turned to see what lay ahead of us.

A dark, high-ceilinged room seemed to stretch on forever. A glass case stood centered in the entryway. Inside was a detailed construction of wood and clay.

I went up close to take a good look. The construction showed thousands of workers dragging enormous blocks of limestone across the sand toward a partially built pyramid.

In the room behind the display I could see huge stone statues, large mummy cases, displays of glass and pottery, and case after case of artifacts and relics.

"I think this is the place!" I exclaimed happily, rushing over to the first display case.

"Ooh, what's that? Some kind of giant dog?" Sari asked, pointing to an enormous statue against the wall.

The creature appeared to have a fierce dog's head and a lion's body. Its eyes stared straight ahead, and it seemed ready to pounce on anyone who came near it.

"They put creatures like that in front of tombs," I told Sari. "You know. To protect the place. Scare away grave robbers."

"Like guard dogs," Sari said, stepping up close to the ancient sculpture.

"Hey — there's a mummy in this case!" I exclaimed, leaning over an ancient stone coffin. "Look!"

Still staring back at the enormous sculpture, Sari walked up beside me. "Yep. It's a mummy, okay," she said, unimpressed. I guess she's seen a lot more of them than me.

"It's so small," I said, staring at the yellowed linen wrapped so tightly around the skinny head and body.

"Our ancestors were shrimps," Sari replied. "Think it was a man or a woman?"

I glanced at the plaque on the side of the coffin. "It says it's a man."

"Guess they didn't work out in those days," she said and laughed at her own remark.

"They did a great wrapping job," I said, examining the carefully wrapped fingers on the hands, which were crossed over the mummy's chest. "I was a mummy the Halloween before last, and my costume completely unraveled after ten minutes!"

Sari tsk-tsked.

"Do you know how they made mummies?" I

asked, moving around to view it from the other side. "Do you know the first thing they did? They removed the brain."

"Yuck. Stop," she said, sticking out her tongue and making a disgusted face.

"Don't you *know* about this?" I asked, delighted that I had some truly gruesome information that she didn't.

"Please — enough," she said, holding up one hand as if to fend me off.

"No, this is interesting," I insisted. "The brain had to come out first. They had this special tool. It was like a long, skinny hook. They'd push it up the corpse's nose until it reached the brain and then wiggled it back and forth, back and forth, until the brain became mush."

"*Stop!*" Sari pleaded, covering her ears.

"Then they took a long spoon," I continued gleefully, "and scooped the brain out a little at a time."

I made a scooping motion with my hand. "Scoop scoop. They scooped the brain out through the nose. Or sometimes they popped off an eyeball and scooped the brain out through the eyeball socket."

"Gabe — I *mean* it!" Sari cried. She really looked like she was about to hurl. She was green!

I loved it.

I never knew that Sari had a squeamish bone in her body. But I was really making her sick.

Outstanding! I thought.

I would definitely have to remember this technique.

"It's all true," I told her, unable to hold back a wide grin.

"Just shut up," she muttered.

"Of course sometimes they didn't pull the brain out the nose. Sometimes they just sliced off the head. Then they drained the brains out through the neck and put the head back on the body. They just bandaged it back on, I guess."

"Gabe — "

I'd been staring at her the whole time, checking out her reaction. She was looking sicker and sicker. She was breathing real heavy. Her chest was sort of heaving. I really thought she was going to lose her breakfast.

If she did, I'd never let her forget it.

"That's really gross," she said. Her voice sounded funny, like it was coming from underwater or something.

"But it's true," I said. "Didn't your dad ever tell you about how they made mummies?"

She shook her head. "He knows I don't like — "

"And you know what they did with the guts?" I asked, enjoying the startled look on her face. "They put them in jars and — "

I suddenly realized that Sari's startled look wasn't for me.

She was actually staring over my shoulder.

"Huh?" I turned around and saw why she suddenly looked so surprised.

A man had entered the room and was standing just in front of the first display case. It took me a few seconds to recognize him.

It was Ahmed, the strange, silent Egyptian with the black ponytail who had greeted us in such an unfriendly manner down inside the pyramid. He was dressed the same, in loose-fitting white trousers and shirt with a scarlet bandanna around his neck. And his expression was just as unfriendly. Angry, even.

Sari and I both backed away from the mummy case, and Ahmed, his eyes darting from one of us to the other, took a step toward us.

"Gabe, he's coming after us!" Sari whispered. She grabbed my arm. Her hand was cold as ice. "Let's get out of here!" she cried.

I hesitated. Shouldn't we stop and say hello to him first?

But something about the stern, determined look on Ahmed's face told me that Sari was right.

We turned and began walking really fast away from him into the vast room, Sari a few steps ahead of me.

I turned and saw that Ahmed was jogging after us.

He shouted something to us, his voice angry, threatening. I couldn't make out the words.

"Run!" Sari cried.

And now we were both running at full speed, our sneakers drumming loudly over the polished marble floor.

We scooted around an enormous glass display case containing three upright mummy cases. Then we ran straight down the wide aisle between sculptures and shelves of ancient pottery and pyramid relics.

Behind us, I could hear Ahmed shouting furiously, "Come back! Come back!"

He sounded really angry.

His shoes clacked against the floor as he ran, the sound echoing in the vast, empty museum chamber.

"He's gaining on us!" I called to Sari, who was still a few steps ahead.

"There's got to be a way *out* of here!" she answered breathlessly.

But I immediately saw that there wasn't. We were nearly to the back wall. We passed a gigantic sphinx, then stopped.

There was nowhere to go.

No doorway. No exit.

A solid granite wall.

We both turned and saw Ahmed's eyes grow wide with triumph.

He had us cornered.

8

Ahmed stopped a few feet in front of us. He was panting like a dog, gasping for air, and holding his side. He glared at us angrily.

Sari glanced at me. She looked pale, really frightened. We both had our backs pressed against the wall.

I swallowed hard. My throat felt tight and dry. What was he going to do to us?

"Why did you run?" Ahmed finally managed to say, still holding his side as if he had a cramp. "Why?"

We didn't reply. We both stared back at him, waiting to see what he was about to do.

"I came with a message from your father," he told Sari, breathing hard. He raised the red bandanna from his neck and wiped his perspiring forehead with it. "Why did you run?"

"A message?" Sari stammered.

"Yes," Ahmed said. "You know me. We met again yesterday. I don't understand why you ran."

"I'm sorry," Sari said quickly, glancing guiltily at me.

"We weren't thinking clearly," I said. "Sari frightened me, and I followed her."

"Gabe was telling me all this frightening stuff," she said, jabbing me hard in the side with her elbow. "It was *his* fault. He scared me with all this mummy stuff. So when I saw you, I wasn't thinking clearly, and . . ."

Both of us were babbling. We both felt so relieved that he wasn't chasing us — and so embarrassed that we had run away from him.

"Your father sent me to get you," Ahmed said, his dark eyes trained on me. "I didn't think I'd have to chase you through the whole museum."

"Sorry," Sari and I said in unison.

I felt like a complete jerk. I'm sure Sari did, too.

"Daddy came back to the hotel and saw Gabe's note?" Sari asked, straightening her hair with her hand as she moved away from the wall.

"Yes." Ahmed nodded.

"He got back from the hospital awfully fast," Sari said, glancing at her wristwatch.

"Yes," Ahmed replied again. "Come. I will take you back to the hotel. He is waiting for you there."

We followed him in silence, Sari and I walking side by side a few steps behind him.

As we made our way down the long stairway, we glanced sheepishly at each other. We were both feeling really foolish for running away like that.

A short while later, we were back on the crowded, noisy sidewalk, an unending stream of cars honking past, all moving in starts and stops, drivers hanging out of car windows, shouting and shaking their fists.

Ahmed checked to make sure we were with him, then turned right and began leading the way through the crowd. The sun was high over the buildings now. The air was hot and humid.

"Hey, wait — " I called.

Ahmed turned back, but kept walking.

"We're going the wrong way," I called to him, shouting over the cries of a street peddler behind a cart of vegetables. "The hotel is back that way." I pointed.

Ahmed shook his head. "My car is just up there."

"We're driving back to the hotel?" Sari asked, her voice revealing her surprise.

"It's only two blocks," I said to Ahmed. "Sari and I could walk back by ourselves if you want. You really don't have to take us."

"It is no trouble," Ahmed replied, and he placed his hands firmly, one on my shoulder, one on Sari's, and continued to guide us to his car.

We crossed the street and continued walking. The sidewalk grew even more crowded. A man swinging a leather briefcase accidentally clipped

61

my shoulder with it. I cried out in pain.

Sari laughed.

"You have a great sense of humor," I muttered sarcastically.

"I know," she replied.

"If we'd walked, we would have been at the hotel already," I said.

Ahmed must have overheard, because he said, "The car's in the next block."

We made our way quickly through the crowds. A short while later, Ahmed stopped at a small, four-door stationwagon. It was covered with dust, and the fender on the driver's side was crunched.

He pulled open the back door, and Sari and I piled in. "Ow," I complained. The leather seats were burning hot.

"The wheel is hot, too," Ahmed said, climbing in and fastening his seat belt. He touched the steering wheel a few times with both hands, trying to get used to the heat. "They should invent a car that stays cool inside when it is parked."

The engine started on the second try, and he pulled away from the curb and into the line of traffic.

Immediately, he began honking the horn at the car in front of us. We moved slowly, stopping every few seconds, through the narrow street.

"I wonder why Daddy didn't come to get us," Sari said to me, her eyes on the crowds passing by the dusty car window.

"He said he would wait for you at the hotel," Ahmed replied from the front seat.

He made a sudden sharp turn onto a wider avenue and began to pick up speed.

It took me a long while to realize that we were heading in the wrong direction — *away* from our hotel. "Uh . . . Ahmed . . . I think the hotel is back that way," I said, pointing toward the back window.

"I believe you are mistaken," he replied softly, staring straight ahead through the windshield. "We will be there shortly."

"No. Really," I insisted.

One thing about me is I have a really good sense of direction. Mom and Dad always say they don't need a map when I'm around. I almost always know when I'm heading the wrong way.

Sari turned to glance at me, an expression of concern beginning to tighten her features.

"Settle back and enjoy the ride," Ahmed said, staring at me through the rearview mirror. "Have you fastened your seat belts? Better do it right now."

He had a smile on his face, but his voice was cold. His words sounded like a threat.

"Ahmed, we've gone too far," I insisted, starting to feel really afraid.

Outside the window, the buildings were lower, more rundown. We seemed to be heading away from the downtown area.

"Just settle back," he replied with growing impatience. "I know where I'm going."

Sari and I exchanged glances. She looked as worried as I did. We both realized that Ahmed was lying to us. He wasn't taking us to the hotel. He was taking us out of town.

We were being kidnapped.

9

Seeing Ahmed's eyes on me in the rearview mirror, I fiddled with the seat belt, pretending to fasten it. As I did this, I leaned close to Sari and whispered in her ear, "Next time he stops."

At first she didn't get my meaning. But then I saw that she understood.

We both sat tensely, eyes on the door handles, waiting in silence.

"Your father is a very smart man," Ahmed said, staring at Sari in the mirror.

"I know," Sari replied in a tiny voice.

The traffic slowed, then stopped.

"Now!" I screamed.

We both grabbed for the door handles.

I pushed my door open and flung myself out of the car.

Horns were honking in front of me and behind me. I could hear Ahmed's surprised shout.

Leaving the car door open, I turned to see that Sari had made it to the street, too. She turned to me as she slammed her door shut, her eyes wide with fear.

Without a word, we started to run.

The car horns seemed to grow louder as we headed into a narrow side street. We were running side by side, following the narrow brick street as it curved between two rows of tall, white stucco buildings.

I feel like a rat in a maze, I thought.

The street grew even narrower. Then it emptied into a wide circle filled with a small market of fruit and vegetable stands.

"Is he following us?" Sari cried, a few steps behind me now.

I turned back and searched for him, my eyes darting through the small crowd attending the market.

I saw several people in flowing white robes. Two women entered the market, dressed in black, carrying a basket loaded high with bananas. A boy on a bicycle swerved to keep from running straight into them.

"I don't see him," I called back to Sari.

But we kept running just to make sure.

I'd never been so scared in my life.

Please, *please*, I begged silently, don't let him be following us. Don't let him catch us!

Turning a corner, we found ourselves on a wide, busy avenue. A truck bounced past, pulling a trailer filled with horses. The sidewalk was crowded with shoppers and businesspeople.

Sari and I pushed our way through them, trying to lose ourselves in the crowd.

Finally, we came to a stop near the entrance of what appeared to be a large department store. Breathing hard, I rested my hands on my knees, leaned forward, and tried to catch my breath.

"We've lost him," Sari said, staring back in the direction from which we'd come.

"Yeah. We're okay," I said happily. I smiled at her, but she didn't return the smile.

Her face was filled with fear. Her eyes continued to stare into the crowd. One hand tugged nervously at a strand of her hair.

"We're okay," I repeated. "We got away."

"There's only one problem," she said quietly, her eyes still on the crowd bustling toward us on the sidewalk.

"Huh? Problem?"

"Now we're lost," she replied, finally turning to face me. "We're lost, Gabe. We don't know where we are."

I suddenly had a heavy feeling in the pit of my stomach. I started to utter a frightened cry.

But I forced myself to hold it in.

I forced myself to pretend I wasn't afraid.

Sari had always been the brave one, the winner, the champ. And I was always the wimp. But now

I could see that she was really scared. This was my chance to be the cool one, my chance to show her who was really the champ.

"No problem," I told her, gazing up at the tall glass and concrete buildings. "We'll just ask somebody to direct us to the hotel."

"But no one speaks English!" she cried, sounding as if she were about to cry.

"Uh . . . no problem," I said, a little less cheerily. "I'm sure someone . . ."

"We're lost," she repeated miserably, shaking her head. "Totally lost."

And then I saw the answer to our problem parked at the curb. It was a taxi, an empty taxi.

"Come on," I said, tugging her arm. I pulled her to the taxi. The driver, a thin, young man with a wide black mustache and stringy black hair falling out of a small gray cap, turned around in surprise as Sari and I climbed into the back seat.

"The Cairo Center Hotel," I said, glancing reassuringly at Sari.

The driver stared back at me blankly, as if he didn't understand.

"Please take us to the Cairo Center Hotel," I repeated slowly and clearly.

And then he tossed back his head, opened his mouth, and started to laugh.

The driver laughed till tears formed in the corners of his eyes.

Sari grabbed my arm. "He's working for Ahmed," she whispered, squeezing my wrist. "We've walked right into a trap!"

"Huh?" I felt a stab of fear in my chest.

I didn't think she was right.

She *couldn't* be right!

But I didn't know what else to think.

I grabbed the door handle and started to leap out of the taxi. But the driver raised a hand, signaling for me to stop.

"Gabe — *go!*" Sari pushed me hard from behind.

"Cairo Center Hotel?" the driver asked suddenly, wiping the tears from his eyes with a finger. Then he pointed through the windshield. "Cairo Center Hotel?"

Sari and I both followed his finger.

There was the hotel. Right across the street.

He started to laugh again, shaking his head.

"Thanks," I shouted, and climbed out.

Sari scrambled out behind me, a wide, relieved smile on her face. "I don't think it's *that* funny," I told her. "The cab driver has a strange sense of humor."

I turned back. The driver was still staring at us, a broad smile on his face.

"Come on," she urged, tugging at my arm. "We have to tell Daddy about Ahmed."

But to our surprise, our hotel room was empty. My note was still on the table where I had left it. Nothing had been moved or touched.

"He hasn't been back here," Sari said, picking up my note and crumpling it into a ball in her hand. "Ahmed lied — about everything."

I flopped down on the couch with a loud sigh. "I wonder what's going on," I said unhappily. "I just don't get it."

Sari and I both screamed as the door to the room flew open.

"Daddy!" Sari cried, running to hug him.

I was sure glad it was Uncle Ben, and not Ahmed.

"Daddy, the strangest thing — " Sari started.

Uncle Ben had his arm around her shoulder. As he led her across the room toward the couch, I could see that he had a really dazed expression on his face.

"Yes, it's strange," he muttered, shaking his head. "Both of my workers . . ."

70

"Huh? Are they okay?" Sari asked.

"No. Not really," Uncle Ben replied, dropping onto the arm of the armchair, staring hard but not really focusing on me. "They're both . . . in a state of shock. I guess that's how to describe it."

"They were in an accident? In the pyramid?" I asked.

Uncle Ben scratched the bald spot at the back of his head. "I don't really know. They can't talk. They're both . . . speechless. I think something — or someone — frightened them. Scared them speechless. The doctors are completely confused. They said that — "

"Daddy, Ahmed tried to kidnap us!" Sari interrupted, squeezing his hand.

"What? Ahmed?" He narrowed his eyes, his forehead wrinkling up in confusion. "What do you mean?"

"Ahmed. The guy at the pyramid. The one who wears the white suits with the red bandanna and always carries the clipboard," Sari explained.

"He told us you sent him to get us," I said. "He came to the museum — "

"Museum?" Uncle Ben climbed to his feet. "What were you doing at the museum? I thought I told you — "

"We had to get out of here," Sari said, putting a hand on her dad's shoulder, trying to calm him. "Gabe wanted to see mummies, so we went to the museum. But Ahmed came and took us to his car.

71

He said he was taking us to you at the hotel."

"But he was driving the wrong way," I continued the story. "So we jumped out and ran away."

"Ahmed?" Uncle Ben kept repeating the name, as if he just couldn't believe it. "He came to me with excellent credentials and references," he said. "He's a cryptographer. He studies ancient Egyptian. He's mainly interested in the wall writings and symbols we uncover."

"So why did he come for us?" I asked.

"Where was he going to take us?" Sari asked.

"I don't know," Uncle Ben said. "But I certainly intend to find out." He hugged Sari. "What a mystery," he continued. "You're both okay?"

"Yeah. We're okay," I replied.

"I've got to get to the pyramid," he said, letting go of Sari and walking to the window. "I gave my workers the day off. But I've got to get to the bottom of this."

Clouds rolled over the sun. The room suddenly grew darker.

"I'll order up some room service for you," Uncle Ben said, a thoughtful expression on his face. "Will you two be okay here till I get back tonight?"

"No!" Sari cried. "You can't leave us here!"

"Why can't we come with you?" I asked.

"Yes! We're coming with you!" Sari exclaimed, before Uncle Ben had a chance to reply.

He shook his head. "Too dangerous," he said, his eyes narrowing as he glanced first at me, then at Sari. "Until I can find out what happened to my two workers in there — "

"But, Daddy, what if Ahmed comes back?" Sari cried, sounding really frightened. "What if he comes here?"

Uncle Ben scowled. "Ahmed," he muttered. "Ahmed."

"You can't leave us here!" Sari repeated.

Uncle Ben stared out the window at the darkening sky. "I guess you're right," he said finally. "I guess I have to take you with me."

"Yes!" Sari and I both cried, relieved.

"But you have to promise to stick close," Uncle Ben said sternly, pointing a finger at Sari. "I mean it. No wandering off. No more practical jokes."

I realized I was seeing a whole new side of my uncle. Even though he was a well-known scientist, he had always been the jolly practical joker of the family.

But now he was worried.

Seriously worried.

No more jokes until the frightening mystery was cleared up.

We had sandwiches downstairs in the hotel restaurant, then drove through the desert to the pyramid.

Heavy clouds rolled across the sun as we drove, casting shadows over the sand, coloring the desert darkly in shimmering shades of blue and gray.

Before long, the enormous pyramid loomed on

the horizon, appearing to grow larger as we approached on the nearly empty highway.

I remembered the first time I had seen it, just a few days before. Such an amazing sight.

But now, watching it through the car windshield, I felt only dread.

Uncle Ben parked the car near the low entrance he had discovered behind the pyramid. As we stepped out, the wind whipped at the ground, tossing the sand up, whirling it around our legs.

Uncle Ben raised a hand to stop us at the tunnel entrance.

"Here," he said. He reached into his supply pack and pulled out equipment for Sari and me. "Clip this on."

He handed each of us a beeper. "Just push the button, and it will beep me," he said, helping me clip mine to the belt on my jeans. "It's like a homing device. If you push the button, it sends electronic signals to the unit I'm wearing. Then I can track you down by following the sound levels. Of course, I don't expect you to use it because I expect you to stay close to me."

He handed us flashlights. "Watch your step," he instructed. "Keep the light down at your feet, a few yards ahead of you on the floor."

"We *know*, Daddy," Sari said. "We've done this before, remember?"

"Just follow instructions," he said sharply, and turned into the darkness of the pyramid opening.

I stopped at the entrance and pulled out my little mummy hand, just to make sure I had it.

"What are you doing with that?" Sari asked, making a face.

"My good luck charm," I said, slipping it back into my pocket.

She groaned and gave me a playful shove into the pyramid entrance.

A few minutes later, we were once again making our way carefully down the long rope ladder and into the first narrow tunnel.

Uncle Ben led the way, the wide circle of light from his flashlight sweeping back and forth across the tunnel ahead of him. Sari was a few steps behind him, and I walked a few steps behind her.

The tunnel seemed narrower and lower this time. I guess it was just my mood.

Gripping the flashlight tightly, keeping the light aimed down, I dipped my head to keep from hitting the low, curved ceiling.

The tunnel bent to the left, then sloped downhill where it split into two paths. We followed the one to the right. The only sound was that of our shoes scraping against the sandy, dry floor.

Uncle Ben coughed.

Sari said something. I couldn't hear what it was.

I had stopped to shine my light on a bunch of spiders on the ceiling, and the two of them had walked several yards ahead of me.

Following my light as it moved over the floor,

I saw that my sneaker had come untied once again.

"Oh, man — not again!"

I stooped to tie it, setting the flashlight on the ground beside me. "Hey — wait up!" I called.

But they had started to argue about something, and I don't think they heard me. I could hear their voices echoing loudly down the long, twisting tunnel, but I couldn't make out their words.

I hurriedly double-knotted the shoe lace, grabbed up the flashlight, and climbed to my feet. "Hey, wait up!" I shouted anxiously.

Where had they gone?

I realized that I couldn't hear their voices anymore.

This *can't* be happening to me again! I thought.

"Hey!" I shouted, cupping my hands over my mouth. My voice echoed down the tunnel.

But no voices called back.

"Wait up!"

Typical, I thought.

They were so involved in their argument, they forgot all about me.

I realized that I was more angry than frightened. Uncle Ben had made such a big deal about us sticking close together. And then he walked off and left me alone in the tunnel.

"Hey, where *are* you?" I shouted.

No reply.

11

Beaming the light ahead of me on the floor, I ducked my head and began jogging, following the tunnel as it curved sharply to the right.

The floor began to slope upwards. The air became hot and musty smelling. I found myself gasping for breath.

"Uncle Ben!" I called. "Sari!"

They must be around the next curve in the tunnel, I told myself. It hadn't taken me that long to tie my shoelace. They couldn't have gotten that far ahead.

Hearing a sound, I stopped.

And listened.

Silence now.

Was I starting to hear things?

I had a sudden flash: Was this another mean practical joke? Were Sari and Uncle Ben hiding, waiting to see what I'd do?

Was this another lame trick of theirs to frighten me?

It could be. Uncle Ben, I knew, could never resist a practical joke. He had laughed like a hyena when Sari told him how she'd hid in the mummy case and scared about ten years off my life.

Were they both hiding in mummy cases now, just waiting for me to stumble by?

My heart thumped in my chest. Despite the heat of the ancient tunnel, I felt cold all over.

No, I decided. This isn't a practical joke.

Uncle Ben was too serious today, too worried about his stricken workers. Too worried about what we'd told him about Ahmed. He wasn't in any mood for practical jokes.

I began making my way through the tunnel again. As I jogged, my hand brushed against the beeper at my waist.

Should I push it?

No, I decided.

That would only give Sari a good laugh. She'd be eager to tell everyone how I'd started beeping for help after being in the pyramid for two minutes!

I turned the corner. The tunnel walls seemed to close in on me as the tunnel narrowed.

"Sari? Uncle Ben?"

No echo. Maybe the tunnel was too narrow for an echo.

The floor grew harder, less sandy. In the dim yellow light, I could see that the granite walls were lined with jagged cracks. They looked like dark lightning bolts coming down from the ceiling.

"Hey — where *are* you guys?" I shouted.

I stopped when the tunnel branched in two directions.

I suddenly realized how scared I was.

Where had they disappeared to? They *had* to have realized by now that I wasn't with them.

I stared at the two openings, shining my light first into one tunnel, then the other.

Which one had they entered?

Which one?

My heart pounding, I ran into the tunnel on the left and shouted their names.

No reply.

I backed out quickly, my light darting wildly over the floor, and stepped into the tunnel to the right.

This tunnel was wider and higher. It curved gently to the right.

A maze of tunnels. That's how Uncle Ben had described the pyramid. Maybe thousands of tunnels, he had told me.

Thousands.

Keep moving, I urged myself.

Keep moving, Gabe.

They're right up ahead. They've *got* to be!

I took a few steps and then called out to them.

I heard something.

Voices?

I stopped. It was so quiet now. So quiet, I could

hear my heart pounding in my chest.

The sound again.

I listened hard, holding my breath.

It was a chattering sound. A soft chittering. Not a human voice. An insect, maybe. Or a rat.

"Uncle Ben? Sari?"

Silence.

I took a few more steps into the tunnel. Then a few more.

I decided I'd better forget my pride and beep them.

So what if Sari teased me about it?

I was too frightened to care.

If I beeped them, they'd be right there to get me in a few seconds.

But as I reached to my waist for the beeper, I was startled by a loud noise.

The insect chittering became a soft *cracking* sound.

I stopped to listen, the fear rising up to my throat.

The soft cracking grew louder.

It sounded like someone breaking saltines in two.

Only louder. Louder.

Louder.

Right under my feet.

I turned my eyes to the floor.

I shined the light at my shoes.

It took me so long to realize what was happening.

The ancient tunnel floor was cracking apart beneath me.

The cracking grew louder, seemed to come from all directions, to surround me.

By the time I realized what was happening, it was too late.

I felt as if I were being pulled down, sucked down by a powerful force.

The floor crumbled away beneath me, and I was falling.

Falling down, down, down an endless black hole.

I opened my mouth to scream, but no sound came out.

My hands flew up and grabbed — nothing!

I closed my eyes and fell.

Down, down into the swirling blackness.

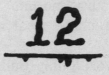

12

I heard the flashlight clang against the floor.

Then I hit. Hard.

I landed on my side. Pain shot through my body, and I saw red. A flash of bright red that grew brighter and brighter until I had to close my eyes. I think the force of the blow knocked me out for a short while.

When I opened my eyes, everything was a gray-yellow blur. My side ached. My right elbow throbbed with pain.

I tried the elbow. It seemed to move okay.

I sat up. The haze slowly began to lift, like a curtain slowly rising.

Where was I?

A sour smell invaded my nostrils. The smell of decay. Of ancient dust. Of death.

The flashlight had landed beside me on the concrete floor. I followed its beam of light toward the wall.

And gasped.

The light stopped on a hand.

A human hand.

Or was it?

The hand was attached to an arm. The arm hung stiffly from an erect body.

My hand trembling, I grabbed up the flashlight and tried to steady the light on the figure.

It was a mummy, I realized. Standing on its feet near the far wall.

Eyeless, mouthless, the bandaged face seemed to stare back at me, tense and ready, as if waiting for me to make the first move.

13

A mummy?

The light darted over its featureless face. I couldn't steady my hand. My whole body was shaking.

Frozen in place, not able to move off the hard floor, I gaped at the frightening figure. I suddenly realized I was panting loudly.

Trying to calm myself, I sucked in a deep breath of the putrid air, and held it.

The mummy stared blindly back at me.

It stood stiffly, its arms hanging at its sides.

Why is it standing there like that? I wondered, taking another deep breath.

The ancient Egyptians didn't leave their mummies standing at attention.

Realizing that it wasn't moving forward to attack me, I began to feel a little calmer.

"Easy, Gabe. Easy," I said aloud, trying to steady the flashlight I gripped so tightly in my hand.

I coughed. The air was so foul. So *old*.

Groaning from the pain in my side, I climbed to my feet and began rapidly shining the light back and forth beyond the silent, faceless mummy.

I was in an enormous, high-ceilinged chamber. Much bigger than the chamber Uncle Ben's workers had been digging in.

And much more cluttered.

"Wow." I uttered a low cry as the pale light of the flashlight revealed an amazing scene. Dark, bandaged figures hovered all around me.

The vast chamber was *crammed* with mummies!

In the unsteady light, their shadows seemed to reach toward me.

Shuddering, I took a step back. I moved the light slowly over the strange, hideous scene.

The light burned through the shadows, revealing bandaged arms, torsos, legs, covered faces.

There were so many of them.

There were mummies leaning against the wall. Mummies lying on stone slabs, arms crossed over their chests. Mummies leaning at odd angles, crouched low or standing tall, their arms straight out in front of them like Frankenstein monsters.

Against one wall stood a row of mummy cases, their lids propped open. I turned, following the arc of my light. I realized that my fall had dropped me into the center of the room.

Behind me, I could make out an amazing array

of equipment. Strange, pronglike tools I had never seen before. Tall stacks of cloth. Gigantic clay pots and jars.

Easy, Gabe. Easy.

Whoa. Breathe slowly.

I took a few reluctant steps closer, trying to hold the flashlight steady.

A few more steps.

I walked up to one of the tall stacks of cloth. Linen, most likely. The material used for making mummies.

Gathering my courage, I examined some of the tools. Not touching anything. Just staring at them in the wavering light of the flashlight.

Mummy-making tools. Ancient mummy-making tools.

I stepped away. Turned back toward the crowd of unmoving figures.

My light traveled across the room and came to rest on a dark square area on the floor. Curious, I moved closer, stepping around twin mummies, lying on their backs, their arms crossed over their chests.

Whoa. Easy, Gabe.

My sneakers scraped noisily along the floor as I made my way hesitantly across the vast chamber.

The dark square on the floor was nearly the size of a swimming pool. I bent down at its edge to examine it more closely.

The surface was soft and sticky. Like tar.

Was this an ancient tar pit? Was this tar used in the making of the mummies that hovered so menacingly around the room?

I had a sudden chill that froze me to the spot.

How could this tar pit be soft after *four thousand years*?

Why was everything in this chamber — the tools, the mummies, the linen — preserved so well?

And why were these mummies — at least two dozen of them — left out like this, scattered about the room in such strange positions?

I realized that I had made an incredible discovery here. By falling through the floor, I had found a hidden chamber, a chamber where mummies had been made. I had found all of the tools and all of the materials used to make mummies four thousand years ago.

Once again, the sour smell invaded my nose. I held my breath to keep myself from gagging. It was the smell of four-thousand-year-old bodies, I realized. A smell that had been bottled up in this ancient, hidden chamber — until now.

Staring at the twisted, shadowy figures gazing back at me in faceless horror, I reached for the beeper.

Uncle Ben, you must come quickly, I thought.

I don't want to be alone down here any longer. You must come here *now*!

I pulled the beeper off my belt and brought it up close to the light.

All I had to do, I realized, was push the button, and Uncle Ben and Sari would come running.

Gripping the small square tightly in my hand, I moved my hand to the button — and cried out in alarm.

The beeper was ruined. Wrecked. Smashed.

The button wouldn't even push.

I must have landed on it when I fell.

It was useless.

I was all alone down here.

Alone with the ancient mummies, staring facelessly, silently, at me through the deep, dark shadows.

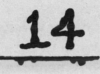

14

All alone.

I stared in horror at the worthless beeper.

The flashlight trembled in my hand.

Suddenly, everything seemed to move in on me. The walls. The ceiling. The darkness.

The mummies.

"Huh?"

I stumbled back a step. Then another.

I realized I was gripping the flashlight so tightly, my hand hurt.

The light played over the faceless figures.

They weren't moving.

Of *course* they weren't moving.

I took another step back. The sour odor seemed to grow stronger, thicker. I held my breath, but the smell was in my nostrils, in my mouth. I could taste it, taste the decay, taste the four-thousand-year-old aroma of death.

I tossed the worthless beeper on the floor and

took another step back, keeping my eyes on the hovering mummies.

What was I going to do?

The smell was making me sick. I had to get out of there, had to call Uncle Ben.

Another step back.

"Help!"

I tried to shout, but my voice sounded weak, muffled by the heavy, foul air.

"Help! Can anybody hear me?" A little louder.

Tucking the flashlight under my arm, I cupped my hands around my mouth to form a megaphone. *"Can anybody hear me?"* I screamed.

I listened, desperate for a reply.

Silence.

Where *were* Sari and Uncle Ben? Why couldn't they hear me? Why weren't they looking for me?

"Help! Somebody — please help!"

I screamed as loud as I could, tilting my head up to the hole in the ceiling, the hole I had fallen through.

"Can't anybody hear me?" I shrieked.

I could feel the panic grip my chest, freeze my legs.

The panic swept over me, wave after paralyzing wave.

"Help me! *Somebody* — please!"

I took another step back.

And something crunched under my sneaker.

I uttered a high-pitched yelp and stumbled forward.

Whatever it was slithered away.

I exhaled loudly, a long sigh of relief.

And then I felt something brush against my ankle.

I cried out, and the flashlight dropped from under my arm. It clattered noisily to the floor.

The light went out.

Again, something scraped silently against me. Something hard.

I heard soft, scrabbling sounds down on the floor. Something snapped at my ankle.

I kicked hard, but hit only air.

"Ohh, help!"

There were creatures down there. A lot of them.

But what *were* they?

Again, something slapped at my ankle, and I kicked wildly.

Frantically, I bent down, grabbing for the flashlight in the darkness.

And touched something hard and warm.

"Ohh, no!"

I jerked my hand up with a startled cry.

In the darkness, groping for the flashlight, I had the feeling that the entire floor had come to life. The floor was moving in waves, rolling and tossing, seething beneath me.

Finally, I found the flashlight. I grabbed it up in my trembling hand, climbed to my feet, and struggled to turn it back on.

As I stepped backward, something slid against my leg.

It felt hard. And prickly.

I heard clicking sounds. Snapping. Creatures bumping into each other.

Panting loudly, my chest heaving, my entire body gripped with terror, I jumped up, tried to dance away as I fiddled with the flashlight.

Something crunched loudly beneath my sneaker. I danced away, hopping over something that scuttled through my legs.

Finally, the light flickered on.

My heart thudding, I lowered the yellow beam of light to the floor.

And saw the scrabbling, snapping creatures.

Scorpions!

I had stumbled into a disgusting nest of them.

"Ohh — help!"

I didn't recognize my tiny, frightened voice as I cried out. I didn't even realize I had cried out.

The light darted over the slithering creatures, their tails raised as if ready to attack, their claws snapping silently as they moved. Crawling over each other. Slithering past my ankles.

"Somebody — help!"

I leapt backwards as a pair of claws grabbed at the leg of my jeans — into another of the creatures whose tail snapped against the back of my sneaker.

Struggling to escape from the poisonous creatures, I tripped.

"No! *Please — no!*"

I couldn't save myself.

I started to fall.

My hands shot out, but there was nothing to grab on to.

I was going to plunge right into the middle of them.

"*Nooooo!*"

I uttered a frantic cry as I toppled forward.

And felt two hands grab me by the shoulders from behind.

15

A mummy! I thought.

My entire body convulsed with fear.

The scorpions snapped and scrabbled at my feet.

The strong hands gripped my shoulders, pulled me hard.

The ancient, bandaged hands.

I couldn't breathe. I couldn't think.

Finally, I managed to spin around.

"Sari!" I cried.

She gave me one more tug. We both stumbled backwards, claws snapping up at us.

"Sari — how — ?"

We moved together now, making our way toward the center of the vast chamber.

Safe. Safe from the disgusting nest of snapping scorpions.

"Saved your life," she whispered. "Yuck. Those are gross!"

"Tell me about it," I said weakly. I could still

feel the hideous creatures sliding along my ankles, still feel them slithering between my legs, crunching under my sneakers.

I don't think I'll ever forget that crunching sound.

"What are you *doing* down here?" Sari cried impatiently, as if scolding a child. "Daddy and I have been looking everywhere for you."

I pulled her even farther from the scorpions, into the center of the chamber. "How did you get down here?" I cried, struggling to calm my breathing, struggling to stop the pounding in my chest.

She pointed with her flashlight to a tunnel in the corner that I hadn't seen. "I was searching for you. Daddy and I got separated. Do you believe it? He stopped to talk to a worker, and I didn't realize it. By the time I turned back, he was gone. Then I saw the light moving around in here. I thought it was Daddy."

"You got lost, too?" I asked, wiping beads of cold sweat off my forehead with the back of my hand.

"I'm not lost. *You're* lost," she insisted. "How could you *do* that, Gabe? Daddy and I were totally freaked."

"Why didn't you wait up for me?" I demanded angrily. "I called to you. You just disappeared."

"We didn't hear you," she replied, shaking her head. I was really glad to see her. But I hated the way she was looking at me, like I was some kind of hopeless idiot. "I guess we got involved in our argument. We thought you were right behind us. Then when we turned around, you were gone." She sighed and shook her head. "What a day!"

"What a day?" I cried shrilly. "What a day?"

"Gabe, why did you *do* that?" she demanded. "You know we were supposed to stay close together."

"Hey — it wasn't my fault," I insisted angrily.

"Daddy is so mad," Sari said, shining her light in my face.

I raised my arm to shield my eyes. "Cut it out," I snapped. "He won't be mad when he sees what I've discovered. Look."

I shined my light onto a mummy crouching near the tar pit, then moved it to another mummy, this one lying down, then to the row of mummy cases against the wall.

"Wow." Sari mouthed the word silently. Her eyes grew wide with surprise.

"Yeah. Wow," I said, starting to feel a little more like normal. "The chamber is filled with mummies. And there are all kinds of tools and cloth and everything you need to make a mummy. It's all in perfect shape, like it hasn't been touched in thousands of years." I couldn't hide my excitement. "And I discovered it all," I added.

"This must be where they prepared the mummies for burial," Sari said, her eyes darting from mummy to mummy. "But why are some of them standing up like that?"

I shrugged. "Beats me."

She walked over to admire the stacks of neatly folded linen. "Wow. This is amazing, Gabe."

"Outstanding!" I agreed. "And if I hadn't stopped to tie my sneaker, I never would have discovered it."

"You're going to be famous," Sari said, a smile spreading across her face. "Thanks to *me* saving your life."

"Sari — " I started.

But she had moved across the room and was admiring one of the upright mummies close up. "Wait till Daddy sees all this," she said, suddenly sounding as excited as me.

"We have to call him," I said eagerly. I glanced back at the scorpion nest and felt a chill of fear tighten the back of my neck.

"People were so tiny back then," she said, holding her flashlight up close to the mummy's covered face. "Look — I'm taller than this one."

"Sari, use your beeper," I said impatiently, walking over to her.

"Yuck. There are bugs crawling in this one's face," she said, stepping back and lowering the light. She made a disgusted face. "Gross."

"Come on. Use your beeper. Call Uncle Ben," I said. I reached for the beeper at her waist, but she pulled away.

"Okay, okay. Why didn't you use *yours*?" She eyed me suspiciously. "You forgot about it, didn't you, Gabe!" she accused.

"No way," I replied sharply. "Mine broke when I fell into this place."

She made a face and pulled the beeper off her belt loop. I shined my light on it as she pushed the button. She pressed it twice, just to make sure, then clipped it back onto her jeans.

We stood with our arms crossed, waiting for Uncle Ben to follow the radio signals and find us.

"It shouldn't take him long," Sari said, her eyes on the tunnel in the corner. "He wasn't far behind me."

Sure enough, a few seconds later, we heard the sounds of someone approaching in the tunnel.

"Uncle Ben!" I called excitedly. "Look what I've found!"

Sari and I both started to run to the tunnel, our lights zigzagging over the low entrance.

"Daddy, you won't believe — " Sari started.

She stopped when the stooped figure leaned out of the darkness and straightened up.

We both gaped in horror, our flashlights making his mustached face glow eerily.

"It's Ahmed!" Sari cried, grabbing my arm.

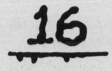

16

I swallowed hard.

Sari and I stared at each other. I saw her features tighten in fear.

Ahmed.

He had tried to kidnap us. And now he had us all alone down here.

He stepped forward, a flaming torch held high in one hand. His black hair glowed in the flickering flames. His eyes narrowed at us in menace.

"Ahmed, what are you doing here?" Sari called, grasping my arm so hard, I winced.

"What are *you* doing here?" he asked softly, his voice as cold as his eyes.

Holding the torch in front of him, he stepped into the chamber. His eyes went around the room, as if inspecting it, making sure that nothing had been moved.

"My dad will be here in a second," Sari warned him. "I just beeped him."

"I tried to warn your father," Ahmed said, staring hard at Sari. The flickering orange light from the torch made him grow bright, then fade into shadow.

"Warn him?" Sari asked.

"About the curse," Ahmed said without emotion.

"Uncle Ben mentioned some kind of curse to me," I said, glancing nervously at Sari. "I don't think he takes that kind of thing seriously."

"He should!" Ahmed replied, screaming the words, his eyes glowing with anger in the torch light.

Sari and I stared back at him in silence.

Where is Uncle Ben? I wondered.

What's keeping him?

Hurry, I urged silently. *Please — hurry!*

"The curse must be carried out," Ahmed said softly again, almost sadly. "I have no choice. You have violated the priestess's chamber."

"Priestess?" I stammered.

Sari was still squeezing my arm. I tugged it away. She crossed her arms resolutely over her chest.

"This chamber belongs to the Priestess Khala," Ahmed said, lowering the torch. "This is the sacred Preparation Chamber of the Priestess Khala, and you have violated it."

"Well, we didn't know," Sari snapped. "I really don't see what's the big deal, Ahmed."

"She's right," I said quickly. "We didn't touch

anything. We didn't move anything. I don't think — "

"*Shut up, you fools!*" Ahmed screamed. He swung the torch angrily as if trying to hit us.

"Ahmed, my dad will be here any second," Sari repeated, her voice trembling.

We both turned our eyes to the tunnel. It was dark and silent.

No sign of Uncle Ben.

"Your father is a smart man," Ahmed said. "It is too bad he wasn't smart enough to heed my warnings."

"Warnings?" Sari asked.

I realized she was stalling for time, trying to keep Ahmed talking until Uncle Ben arrived.

"I frightened the two workers," Ahmed confessed to Sari. "I frightened them to show your father that the curse was alive, that I was prepared to carry out Khala's wishes."

"How did you frighten them?" Sari demanded.

He smiled. "I gave them a little demonstration. I showed them what it might feel like to be boiled alive." He turned his eyes to the tar pit. "They didn't like it," he added quietly.

"But, Ahmed — " Sari started.

He cut her off. "Your father should have known better than to return here. He should have believed me. He should have believed in the Priestess's curse. The Priestess cursed all who would violate her chamber."

"But, come on, you don't really believe — " I started.

He raised the torch menacingly. "It was decreed by Khala more than four thousand years ago that this sacred chamber would not be violated," he cried, gesturing with the torch, leaving a trail of orange light against the darkness. "Since that time, from generation to generation, descendants of Khala have made sure that the Priestess's command was obeyed."

"But, Ahmed — " Sari cried.

"It has come to me," he continued, ignoring her, ignoring us both, staring at the ceiling as he spoke, as if speaking directly to the Priestess up in the heavens. "It has come to me as a descendant of Khala to make sure the curse is carried out."

I stared past Ahmed to the tunnel. Still no sign of Uncle Ben.

Was he coming? Had Sari's beeper worked?

What was keeping him?

"I volunteered to work for your father to make sure that Khala's sacred sanctuary was not violated," Ahmed continued, shadows flickering over his menacing face. "When he would not heed my warnings, I had to take action. I frightened the two workers. Then I planned to take you away, to hide you until he agreed to stop his work."

He lowered the torch. His face filled with sadness. "Now, I have no choice. I must carry out

102

my sacred duties. I must keep the ancient promise to Khala."

"But what does that *mean?*" Sari cried. The orange torchlight revealed her frightened expression.

"What does it mean?" Ahmed repeated. He gestured with the torch. "Look around you."

We both turned and glanced quickly around the chamber. But we didn't understand.

"The mummies," he explained.

We still didn't understand. "What about the mummies?" I managed to stammer.

"They were all violators of the Priestess's chamber," Ahmed revealed. The thin smile that formed on his face could only be described as a proud smile.

"You mean — they're not from ancient Egypt?" Sari cried, raising her hands in horror to her face.

"A few of them," Ahmed replied, still smiling that frightening, cold smile. "A few of them were ancient intruders. Some are quite recent. But they all have one thing in common. They all became victims of the curse. And they all were mummified *alive!*"

"No!" I screamed without realizing it.

Ahmed ignored my terrified outburst. "I did that one myself," he said, pointing to a mummy standing stiffly at attention at the edge of the tar pit.

"Oh, how awful!" Sari cried, her voice trembling.

I stared hopefully at the tunnel opening behind Ahmed. But there was still no sign of Uncle Ben.

"Today, I must go to work again," Ahmed announced. Today there will be new mummies. New trophies for Khala."

"You can't *do* that!" Sari shrieked.

I grabbed her hand.

To my horror, I understood perfectly now. I understood why some of the mummies were in such good condition.

They were new.

All of the tools, the tar, the linen — they had been used by descendants of Khala, descendants like Ahmed. Since the time of Khala, anyone who had entered the chamber — the chamber we were now standing in — had been mummified.

Alive.

And now Sari and I were about to become mummies, too.

"Ahmed, you *can't!*" Sari cried. She let go of my hand and balled her hands into angry fists at her side.

"It is the will of Khala," he replied softly, his dark eyes glowing in the light of the torch.

I saw a long-bladed dagger appear in his free hand. The blade caught the light from the torch.

Sari and I both took a step back as Ahmed began moving toward us with quick, determined strides.

17

As Ahmed approached, Sari and I shrank back to the center of the chamber.

Run, I thought.

We can run away from him.

My eyes searched frantically for a place we could escape through.

But there was no way out.

The tunnel in the corner appeared to be the only opening. And we'd have to run right past Ahmed to get to it.

Sari, I saw, was frantically pressing the beeper at her waist. She glanced at me, her features tight with fear.

"Yowwww!"

I cried out as I suddenly backed into someone.

I turned and stared into the bandaged face of a mummy.

With a loud gasp, I lurched away from it.

"Let's make a run for the tunnel," I whispered

to Sari, my throat so dry and tight, I could barely make myself heard. "He can't get both of us."

Sari stared back at me, confused. I don't know if she heard me or not.

"There is no escape," Ahmed said softly, as if reading my thoughts. "There is no escape from Khala's curse."

"He — he's going to *kill* us!" Sari screamed.

"You have violated her sacred chamber," Ahmed said, raising the torch high, holding the dagger at his waist.

He stepped nearer. "I saw you yesterday climb into the sacred sarcophagus. I saw you two *playing* in Khala's holy chamber. It was then that I knew I had to carry out my sacred duties. I — "

Sari and I both cried out as something dropped from the chamber ceiling.

All three of us looked up to see a rope ladder dangling from the hole I had fallen through. It swung back and forth as it was lowered, nearly to the floor.

"Are you down there? I'm coming down!" Uncle Ben shouted down to us.

"Uncle Ben — no!" I screamed.

But he was already moving down the ladder, making his way quickly, the ladder steadying under his weight.

Halfway down, he stopped and peered into the chamber. "What on earth — ?" he cried, his eyes roaming over the amazing scene.

And then he saw Ahmed.

"Ahmed, what are *you* doing here?" Uncle Ben cried in surprise. He quickly lowered himself to the floor, jumping down the last three rungs.

"Merely carrying out Khala's wishes," Ahmed said, his face expressionless now, his eyes narrowed in anticipation.

"Khala? The Priestess?" Uncle Ben wrinkled his features in confusion.

"He's going to kill us!" Sari cried, rushing up to her dad, throwing her arms around his waist. "Daddy — he's going to kill us! And then turn us into *mummies!*"

Uncle Ben held Sari and looked over her shoulder accusingly at Ahmed. "Is this true?"

"The chamber has been violated. It has fallen to me, Doctor, to carry out the curse."

Uncle Ben put his hands on Sari's trembling shoulders and gently moved her aside. Then he began to make his way slowly, steadily, toward Ahmed.

"Ahmed, let us go out of here and discuss this," he said, raising his right hand as if offering it in friendship.

Ahmed took a step back, raising the torch menacingly. "The Priestess's will must not be ignored."

"Ahmed, you are a scientist, and so am I," Uncle Ben said. I couldn't believe how calm he sounded. I wondered if it was an act.

107

The scene was tense. We were in such terrifying danger.

But I felt just a little bit calmer knowing that my uncle was here, knowing that he'd be able to handle Ahmed and get us out of here — alive.

I glanced reassuringly at Sari, who was staring hard, biting her lower lip in tense concentration as her father approached Ahmed.

"Ahmed, put down the torch," Uncle Ben urged, his hand extended. "The dagger, too. Please. Let's discuss this, scientist to scientist."

"What is there to discuss?" Ahmed asked softly, his eyes studying Uncle Ben intently. "The will of Khala must be carried out, as it has been for four thousand years. That cannot be discussed."

"As scientist to scientist," Uncle Ben repeated, returning Ahmed's stare as if challenging him. "The curse is ancient. Khala has had her way for many centuries. Perhaps it is time to let it rest. Lower your weapons, Ahmed. Let's talk about this. Scientist to scientist."

It's going to be okay, I thought, breathing a long sigh of relief. It's all going to be okay. We're going to get out of here.

But then Ahmed moved with startling quickness.

Without warning, without a word, he pulled back his arms and, gripping the torch handle with both hands, swung it as hard as he could at Uncle Ben's head.

The torch made a loud *thonk* as it connected with the side of Uncle Ben's face.

The orange flames danced up.

A swirl of bright color.

And then shadows.

Uncle Ben groaned. His eyes bulged wide with surprise.

With pain.

The torch hadn't set him aflame. But the blow knocked him out.

He slumped to his knees. Then his eyes closed, and he dropped limply to the floor.

Ahmed raised the torch high, his eyes gleaming with excitement, with triumph.

And I knew we were doomed.

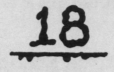

18

"Daddy!"

Sari rushed to her father and knelt at his side.

But Ahmed moved quickly, thrusting the torch toward her, holding the dagger ready, forcing her to back away.

A thin trickle of blood, glowing darkly in the light of the fire, rolled down the side of Uncle Ben's face. He groaned, but didn't stir.

I glanced quickly at the mummies scattered around the room. It was hard to believe that we would soon be one of them.

I thought of leaping at Ahmed, trying to knock him over. I imagined grabbing the torch, swinging it at him, forcing him against the wall. Forcing him to let us escape.

But the blade of the dagger glowed, as if warning me to stay back.

I'm just a kid, I thought.

Thinking I could beat a grown man with a knife and a torch was just crazy.

Crazy.

The whole scene was crazy. And terrifying.

I suddenly felt sick. My stomach tightened, and a wave of nausea swept over me.

"Let us go — *now!*" Sari screamed at Ahmed.

To my surprise, he reacted by swinging back the torch and heaving it across the room.

It landed with a soft *plop* in the center of the tar pit. Instantly, the surface of the tar burst into flames. The flames spread, leaping up toward the chamber ceiling, until the entire square was aflame.

As I stared in amazement, the tar popped and bubbled beneath the orange and red covering of flames.

"We must wait for it to boil," Ahmed said calmly, the shadows cast by the flames flickering across his face and clothing.

The chamber grew thick with smoke. Sari and I both started to cough.

Ahmed bent down and put his hands under Uncle Ben's shoulders. He began to drag him across the floor.

"Leave him alone!" Sari screamed, running frantically toward Ahmed.

I saw that she was going to try to fight him.

I grabbed her shoulders and held her back.

We were no match for Ahmed. He had already knocked Uncle Ben unconscious. There was no telling what he would do to us.

Holding onto Sari, I stared at him. What did he plan to do now?

It didn't take long to find out.

With surprising strength, he pulled Uncle Ben across the floor to one of the open mummy cases against the wall. Then he hoisted him over the side and shoved him into the case. Not even the slightest bit out of breath, Ahmed slid the lid closed over my unconscious uncle.

Then he turned to us. "You two — into that one." He pointed to an enormous mummy case on a tall pedestal next to Uncle Ben's. It was nearly as tall as I was, and at least ten feet long. It must have been built to hold a mummified person — and all of his or her possessions.

"Let us go!" Sari insisted. "Let us out of here. We won't tell anyone what happened. Really!"

"Please climb into the case," Ahmed insisted patiently. "We must wait for the tar to be ready."

"We're not going in there," I said.

I was shaking all over. I could feel the blood pulsing at my temples. I didn't even realize I was saying what I was saying. I was so scared, I didn't even hear myself.

I glanced at Sari. She stood defiantly with her arms crossed tightly over her chest. But despite her brave pose, I could see her chin trembling and her eyes beginning to tear.

"Into the coffin," Ahmed repeated, "to await your fate. Khala will not be kept waiting. The ancient curse will be carried out in her name."

"No!" I cried angrily.

I stood on tiptoe and peered into the enormous mummy case. It smelled so sour in there, I nearly hurled.

The case was made of wood. It was warped and stained and peeling inside. In the flickering light, I was sure I saw dozens of insects crawling around in there.

"Get into the case *now*!" Ahmed demanded.

19

Sari climbed up over the side and lowered herself into the ancient mummy case. She always had to be first at everything. But this was one time I didn't mind.

I hesitated, resting my hand on the rotting wood on the side of the case. I glanced at the case next to it, the case with Uncle Ben inside. It was carved of stone, and the heavy stone lid was closed, sealing it up tight.

Did Uncle Ben have any air in there? I wondered, gripped with fear. Was he able to breathe?

And, then, I thought glumly, what difference does it make? All three of us are going to be dead soon. All three of us are going to be mummies, locked away in this hidden chamber forever.

"Get in — now!" Ahmed ordered, his dark eyes burning into mine.

"I — I'm just a *kid!*" I cried. I don't know where the words came from. I was so scared, I really didn't know what I was saying.

An unpleasant sneer formed on Ahmed's face. "Many of the pharaohs were your age at death," he said.

I wanted to keep him talking. I had the desperate idea that if I could keep the conversation going, I could get us out of this mess.

But I couldn't think of anything to say. My brain just froze.

"Get in," Ahmed ordered, moving toward me menacingly.

Feeling totally defeated, I slid one leg over the side of the rotting coffin, raised myself up, and then dropped down beside Sari.

She had her head bowed, and her eyes shut tight. I think she was praying. She didn't glance up, even when I touched her shoulder.

The coffin lid began to slide over us. The last thing I saw were the red flames leaping up over the pit of tar. Then the lid closed us into complete blackness.

"Gabe . . ." Sari whispered a few seconds after the lid was closed. "I'm frightened."

For some reason, her confession made me snicker. She said it with such *surprise*. As if being frightened was a startling new experience.

"I'm too frightened to be frightened," I whispered back.

She grabbed my hand and squeezed it. Her hand was even colder and clammier than mine.

"He's crazy," she whispered.

"Yeah. I know," I replied, still holding onto her hand.

"I think there are bugs in here," she said with a shudder. "I can feel them crawling on me."

"Me, too," I told her. I realized I was gritting my teeth. I always do that when I'm nervous. And now I was more nervous than I thought was humanly possible.

"Poor Daddy," Sari said.

The air in the coffin was already beginning to feel stuffy and hot. I tried to ignore the disgusting sour smell, but it had crept into my nostrils, and I could even taste it. I held my breath to keep from gagging.

"We're going to suffocate in here," I said glumly.

"He's going to kill us before we can suffocate," Sari wailed. "Ow!" I could hear her slap at a bug on her arm.

"Maybe something will happen," I told her. Pretty lame. But I couldn't think of what else to say. I couldn't *think*. Period.

"All I keep thinking about is how he's going to reach in and pull my brain out through my nose," Sari wailed. "Why did you have to tell me that, Gabe?"

It took me a while to reply. Then, all I could say was, "Sorry." I began to picture the same thing, and another wave of nausea swept over me.

"We can't just sit here," I said. "We have to

escape." I tried to ignore the thick, sour smell.

"Huh? How?"

"Let's try to push up the lid," I said. "Maybe if we both push together . . ."

I counted to three in a low whisper, and we both flattened our hands against the coffin top and pushed up as hard as we could.

No. The lid wouldn't budge.

"Maybe he's locked it or put something heavy on top of it," Sari suggested with a miserable sigh.

"Maybe," I replied, feeling just as miserable.

We sat in silence for a while. I could hear Sari breathing. She was sort of sobbing as she breathed. I realized my heart was racing. I could feel my temples throbbing.

I pictured the long hook that Ahmed would use to pull our brains out of our heads. I tried to force the thought out of my mind, but it wouldn't go away.

I remembered being a mummy two Halloweens ago, and how the costume unraveled in front of my friends.

Little did I know then that I'd soon have a mummy costume that would *never* unravel.

Time passed. I don't know how long.

I realized I had been sitting with my legs crossed. Now they were beginning to fall asleep. I uncrossed them and stretched them out. The mummy case was so big, Sari and I could both lie down if we wanted to.

But we were too tense and terrified to lie down.

I was the first to hear the scrabbling sound. Like something climbing quickly around inside the mummy case.

At first I thought it was Sari. But she grabbed my hand with her icy hand, and I realized she hadn't moved from in front of me.

We both listened hard.

Something near us, something right next to us, bumped the side of the case.

A mummy?

Was there a mummy in the case with us?

Moving?

I heard a soft groan.

Sari squeezed my hand so tightly, it hurt, and I uttered a sharp cry.

Another sound. Closer.

"Gabe — " Sari whispered, her voice tiny and shrill. "Gabe — there's *something* in here with us!"

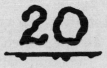

20

It's not a mummy, I told myself.

It *can't* be.

It's a bug. A very large bug. Moving across the coffin floor.

It's not a mummy. It's not a mummy.

The words repeated in my mind.

I didn't have too long to think about it. Whatever it was crept closer.

"Hey!" a voice whispered.

Sari and I both shrieked.

"Where *are* you guys?"

We recognized the voice immediately.

"Uncle Ben!" I cried, swallowing hard, my heart pounding.

"Daddy!" Sari lunged over me to get to her father.

"But how?" I stammered. "How did you get in here?"

"Easy," he replied, squeezing my shoulder reassuringly.

"Daddy — I don't *believe* it!" Sari wailed. I couldn't see in the blackness of the closed coffin, but I think she was crying.

"I'm okay. I'm okay," he repeated several times, trying to calm her down.

"How did you get out of that case and into this one?" I asked, totally confused and amazed.

"There's an escape hatch," Uncle Ben explained. "A small opening with a doorway. The Egyptians built hidden doorways and escape hatches into many of their mummy cases. For the corpse's soul to be able to leave."

"Wow," I said. I didn't know *what* to say.

"Ahmed is so caught up in his ancient curse mumbo jumbo, he's forgotten about this little detail," Uncle Ben said. I felt his hand on my shoulder again. "Come on, you two. Follow me."

"But he's out there — " I started.

"No," Uncle Ben replied quickly. "He's slipped away. When I climbed out of my case, I looked for him. I didn't see him anywhere. Maybe he went somewhere else while he's waiting for the tar to get hot enough. Or maybe he decided to just leave us in the mummy cases to suffocate."

I felt a bug slither up my leg. I slapped at it, then tried to pull it out from inside the leg of my jeans.

"Out we go," Uncle Ben said.

I heard him groan as he turned in the enormous

coffin. Then I could hear him crawling to the back.

I saw a small rectangle of light as he pushed open the hidden door in the back of the case. It was a very small escape hatch, just big enough for us to squeeze through.

I followed Uncle Ben and Sari out of the case, flattening myself to crawl out the small opening, then dropping onto all fours on the chamber floor.

It took a while for my eyes to adjust to the brightness.

The red flames still danced over the pit of bubbling tar, casting eerie blue shadows on all four chamber walls. The mummies stood as before, frozen in place around the room, shadows flickering over their faceless forms.

As my eyes began to focus, I saw that Uncle Ben had an enormous, dark bruise on the side of his head. A wide ribbon of dried blood streaked down his cheek.

"Let's get out of here before Ahmed comes back," he whispered, standing between us, one hand on each of our shoulders.

Sari looked pale and trembly. Her lower lip was bleeding from her chewing on it so hard.

Uncle Ben started toward the rope ladder in the center of the chamber, but then stopped. "It'll take too long," he said, thinking out loud. "Come on. To the tunnel. Hurry."

All three of us started jogging toward the tunnel in the corner. Looking down, I saw that my stupid shoelace had come untied again. But there was *no way* I was going to stop to tie it!

We were about to get *out* of there!

A few seconds before, I had given up all hope. But now, here we were out of the mummy case and heading to freedom.

We were just a few yards in front of the tunnel entrance when the tunnel suddenly filled with orange light.

Then, from out of the tunnel, Ahmed emerged, holding a new torch in front of him, the flames revealing a startled look on his face.

"No!" Sari and I cried in unison.

All three of us skidded to a halt right in front of him.

"You cannot escape!" Ahmed said softly, quickly regaining his composure, his startled expression tightening to anger. "You *will not* escape!"

He thrust the torch toward Uncle Ben, who was forced to fall backwards, out of reach of the hissing flames. He landed hard on his elbows and cried out in pain.

His cry brought a grim smile to Ahmed's lips. "You have made Khala angry," he announced, raising the torch above his head and reaching for the dagger sheathed at his waist. "You will not join the other violators of this chamber."

Whew. I breathed a sigh of relief.

Ahmed had changed his mind. He wasn't going to turn us into mummies after all.

"The three of you will die in the tar pit," he declared.

Sari and I exchanged horrified glances. Uncle Ben had climbed back to his feet and put his arms around us. "Ahmed, can't we talk about this calmly and rationally as scientists?" he asked.

"To the tar pit," Ahmed ordered, thrusting the flaming torch angrily at us.

"Ahmed — *please!*" Uncle Ben cried in a whining, frightened tone I'd never heard from him before.

Ahmed ignored Uncle Ben's desperate pleas. Pushing the torch at our backs and gesturing with the long-bladed dagger, he forced us to make our way to the edge of the pit.

The tar was bubbling noisily now, making ugly popping and sucking sounds. The flames across the top were low and red.

I tried to pull back. It smelled so bad. And the steam coming off it was so hot, it made my face burn.

"One by one, you will jump," Ahmed said.

He was standing a few feet behind us as we stared down into the bubbling tar. "If you don't jump, I will be forced to push you."

"Ahmed — " Uncle Ben began. But Ahmed brushed the torch against Ben's back.

"It has come to me," Ahmed said solemnly. "The

123

honor of carrying out Khala's wishes."

The tar fumes were so overwhelming, I thought I was going to faint. The pit started to tilt in front of me. I felt very dizzy.

I shoved my hands into my jeans pockets, to steady myself, I guess. And my hand closed around something I had forgotten about.

The Summoner.

The mummy hand that I carry around everywhere.

I'm not sure why — I wasn't thinking clearly, if at all — but I pulled out the little mummy hand.

I spun around quickly. And I held the mummy hand up high.

I can't really explain what was going through my mind. I was so terrified, so overwhelmed with fear, that I was thinking a hundred things at once.

Maybe I thought the mummy hand would distract Ahmed.

Or interest him.

Or confuse him.

Or frighten him.

Maybe I was just stalling for time.

Or maybe I was unconsciously remembering the legend behind the hand that the kid at the garage sale had told me.

The legend of why it was called The Summoner.

How it was used to call up ancient souls and spirits.

Or maybe I wasn't thinking anything at all.

But I spun around and, gripping it by its slender wrist, held the mummy hand up high.

And waited.

Ahmed stared at it.

But nothing happened.

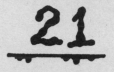

21

I waited, standing there like the Statue of Liberty with the little hand raised high above my head.

It seemed as if I were standing like that for hours.

Sari and Uncle Ben stared at the hand.

Lowering the torch a few inches, Ahmed squinted at the mummy hand. Then his eyes grew wider, and his mouth dropped open in surprise.

He cried out. I couldn't understand what he was saying. The words were in a language I'd never heard. Ancient Egyptian, maybe.

He took a step back, his surprised expression quickly replaced by a wide-eyed look of fear.

"The hand of the Priestess!" he cried.

At least, that's what I *think* he cried — because I was suddenly distracted by what was going on behind him.

Sari uttered a low cry.

All three of us stared over Ahmed's shoulder in disbelief.

A mummy propped against the wall appeared to lean forward.

Another mummy, lying on its back, slowly sat up, creaking as it raised itself.

"No!" I cried, still holding the mummy hand high.

Sari and Uncle Ben were gaping wide-eyed as the vast chamber filled with motion. As the mummies creaked and groaned to life.

The air filled with the odor of ancient dust, of decay.

In the shadowy light, I saw one mummy, then another, straighten up, stand tall. They stretched their bandaged arms above their featureless heads. Slowly. Painfully.

Staggering, moving stiffly, the mummies lumbered forward.

I watched, frozen in amazement, as they climbed out of mummy cases, raised themselves from the floor, leaned forward, took their first slow, heavy steps, their muscles groaning, dust rising up from their dry, dead bodies.

They're dead, I thought.

All of them. Dead. Dead for so many years.

But now they were rising up, climbing from their ancient coffins, struggling toward us on their heavy, dead legs.

Their bandaged feet scraped across the chamber floor as they gathered in a group.

Scrape. Scrape. Scrape.

A dry, shuffling sound I knew I'd never forget. *Scrape. Scrape.*

The faceless army approached. Bandaged arms outstretched, they lumbered toward us, creaking and groaning. Moaning softly with ancient pain.

Ahmed caught the astonishment on our faces and spun around.

He cried out again in that strange language as he saw the mummies advancing on us, scraping so softly, so deliberately, across the chamber floor.

And, then, with a furious scream, Ahmed heaved the torch at the mummy in the lead.

The torch hit the mummy in the chest and bounced to the floor. Flames burst from the mummy's chest, immediately spreading over the arms and down the legs.

But the mummy kept advancing, didn't slow, didn't react at all to the fire that was quickly consuming it.

Gaping in openmouthed horror, babbling an endless stream of words in that mysterious language, Ahmed tried to run.

But he was too late.

The burning mummy lunged at him. The ancient figure caught Ahmed up by the throat, lifted him high above its flaming shoulders.

Ahmed uttered a high-pitched shriek of terror as the other mummies lumbered forward. Moaning and wailing through their yellowed bandages, they moved in to help their burning colleague.

They raised Ahmed high above their moaning heads.

And then held him over the burning tar pit.

Squirming and kicking, Ahmed uttered a piercing scream as they held him over the boiling, bubbling, steaming tar.

I closed my eyes. The heat and tar fumes swirled around me. I felt as if I were being swallowed up, pulled down into the steaming blackness.

When I opened my eyes, I saw Ahmed fleeing to the tunnel, staggering clumsily, shrieking in openmouthed terror as he ran. The mummies remained by the pit, enjoying their victory.

I realized I was still holding the mummy hand over my head. I lowered it slowly, and gazed at Sari and Uncle Ben. They were standing beside me, their faces filled with confusion. And relief.

"The mummies — " I managed to utter.

"Look," Sari said, pointing.

I followed the direction of her gaze. The mummies were all back in place. Some were leaning, some propped at odd angles, some lying down.

They were exactly as they had been when I entered the chamber.

"Huh?" My eyes darted rapidly around the room.

Had they all moved? Had they raised them-selves, stood up, and staggered toward us? Or had we imagined it all?

No.

We *couldn't* have imagined it.

Ahmed was gone. We were safe.

"We're okay," Uncle Ben said gratefully, throwing his arms around Sari and me. "We're okay. We're okay."

"We can go now!" Sari cried happily, hugging her dad. Then she turned to me. "You saved our lives," she said. She had to choke out the words. But she said them.

Then Uncle Ben turned his gaze on me and the object I still gripped tightly in front of me. "Thanks for the helping hand," Uncle Ben said.

We had an enormous dinner at a restaurant back in Cairo. It's a miracle any of us got any food down since we were all talking at once, chattering excitedly, reliving our adventure, trying to make sense of it all.

I was spinning The Summoner around on the table.

Uncle Ben grinned at me. "I had no idea *how* special that mummy hand was!"

He took it from me and examined it closely. "Better not play with it," he said seriously. "We must treat it carefully." He shook his head. "Some great scientist *I* am!" he exclaimed scornfully.

"When I saw it, I thought it was just a toy, some kind of reproduction. But this hand may be my biggest discovery of all!"

"It's my good luck charm," I said, handling it gently as I took it back.

"You can say *that* again!" Sari said appreciatively. The nicest thing she'd ever said to me.

Back at the hotel, I surprised myself by falling asleep instantly. I thought I'd be up for hours, thinking about all that had happened. But I guess all the excitement had exhausted me.

The next morning, Sari, Uncle Ben, and I had a big breakfast in the room. I had a plate of scrambled eggs and a bowl of Frosted Flakes. As I ate, I fiddled with the little mummy hand.

All three of us were feeling good, happy that our frightening adventure was over. We were kidding around, teasing each other, laughing a lot.

After I finished my cereal, I raised the little mummy hand high. "O, Summoner," I chanted in a deep voice, "I summon the ancient spirits. Come alive. Come alive again!"

"Stop it, Gabe," Sari snapped. She grabbed for the hand, but I swung it out of her reach.

"That isn't funny," she said. "You shouldn't fool around like that."

"Are you chicken?" I asked, laughing at her. I could see that she was really frightened, which made me enjoy my little joke even more.

Keeping it away from her, I raised the hand

high. "I summon thee, ancient spirits of the dead,"
I chanted. "Come to me. Come to me now!"

And there was a loud knock on the door.

All three of us gasped.

Uncle Ben knocked over his juice glass. It clattered onto the table and spilled.

I froze with the little hand in the air.

Another loud knock.

We heard a scrabbling at the door. The sound of ancient, bandaged fingers struggling with the lock.

Sari and I exchanged horrified glances.

I slowly lowered the hand as the door swung open.

Two shadowy figures lumbered into the room.

"Mom and Dad!" I cried.

I'll bet they were surprised at how glad I was to see them.

Add *more*

Goosebumps

to your collection . . .
A chilling preview of
what's next from
R.L. STINE

LET'S GET INVISIBLE!

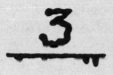

I found myself in a small, windowless room. The only light came from the pale yellow ceiling light behind us in the center of the attic.

"Push the door all the way open so the light can get in," I instructed Erin. "I can't see a thing in here."

Erin pushed open the door and slid a carton over to hold it in place. Then she and April crept in to join Lefty and me.

"It's too big to be a closet," Erin said, her voice sounding even squeakier than usual. "So what is it?"

"Just a room, I guess," I said, still waiting for my eyes to adjust to the dim light.

I took another step into the room. And as I did, a dark figure stepped toward me.

I screamed and jumped back.

The other person jumped back, too.

"It's a mirror, dork!" Lefty said, and started to laugh.

Instantly, all four of us were laughing. Nervous, high-pitched laughter.

It *was* a mirror in front of us. In the pale yellow light filtering into the small, square room, I could see it clearly now.

It was a big, rectangular mirror, about two feet taller than me, with a dark wood frame. It rested on a wooden base.

I moved closer to it and my reflection moved once again to greet me. To my surprise, the reflection was clear. No dust on the glass, despite the fact that no one had been in here in ages.

I stepped in front of it and started to check out my hair.

I mean, that's what mirrors are for, right?

"Who would put a mirror in a room all by itself?" Erin asked. I could see her dark reflection in the mirror, a few feet behind me.

"Maybe it's a valuable piece of furniture or something," I said, reaching into my jeans pocket for my comb. "You know. An antique."

"Did your parents put it up here?" Erin asked.

"I don't know," I replied. "Maybe it belonged to my grandparents. I just don't know." I ran the comb through my hair a few times.

"Can we go now? This isn't too thrilling," April said. She was still lingering reluctantly in the doorway.

"Maybe it was a carnival mirror," Lefty said, pushing me out of the way and making faces into the mirror, bringing his face just inches from the glass. "You know. One of those fun house mirrors that makes your body look like it's shaped like an egg."

"You're already shaped like an egg," I joked, pushing him aside. "At least, your head is."

"You're a *rotten* egg," he snapped back. "You stink."

I peered into the mirror. I looked perfectly normal, not distorted at all. "Hey, April, come in," I urged. "You're blocking most of the light."

"Can't we just leave?" she asked, whining. Reluctantly, she moved from the doorway, taking a few small steps into the room. "Who cares about an old mirror, anyway?"

"Hey, look," I said, pointing. I had spotted a light attached to the top of the mirror. It was oval-shaped, made of brass or some other kind of metal. The bulb was long and narrow, almost like a fluorescent bulb, only shorter.

I gazed up at it, trying to figure it out in the dim light. "How do you turn it on, I wonder."

"There's a chain," Erin said, coming up beside me.

Sure enough, a slender chain descended from the right side of the lamp, hanging down about a foot from the top of the mirror.

"Wonder if it works," I said.

"The bulb's probably dead," Lefty remarked. Good old Lefty. Always an optimist.

"Only one way to find out," I said. Standing on tiptoes, I stretched my hand up to the chain.

"Be careful," April warned.

"Huh? It's just a light," I told her.

Famous last words.

I reached up. Missed. Tried again. I grabbed the chain on the second try and pulled.

The light came on with a startlingly bright flash. Then it dimmed down to normal light. Very white light that reflected brightly in the mirror.

"Hey — that's better!" I exclaimed. "It lights up the whole room. Pretty bright, huh?"

No one said anything.

"I *said*, pretty bright, huh?"

Still silence from my companions.

I turned around and was surprised to find looks of horror on all three faces.

"Max?" Lefty cried, staring hard at me, his eyes practically popping out of his head.

"Max — where are you?" Erin cried. She turned to April. "Where'd he go?"

"I'm right here," I told them. "I haven't moved."

"But we can't see you!" April cried.

About the Author

R.L. STINE is the author of more than two dozen best-selling thrillers and mysteries for young people. Recent titles for teenagers include *Beach House, Hit and Run,* and *The Baby-sitter II,* all published by Scholastic. He is also author of the *Fear Street* series.

When he isn't writing scary books, he is head writer of the children's TV show *Eureeka's Castle,* seen on Nickelodeon.

Bob lives in New York City with his wife, Jane, and twelve-year-old son, Matt.

GET Goosebumps

by R.L Stine
NOW!